The Red of His Shadow

For José Francisco Alegría
and Soraya Aracena,
who led me to Similá

And for my unforgettable
June C. Rosenberg, who chose to live
in the Gagá and for the Gagá

Papá Lokó ou sé van,
pousé-n alé
nou sé papiyon
na poté nouvel bay agoué . . .

(Papa Lokó, you are the wind,
blow on us, we are
butterflies, and we will carry
the news to the others . . .)

—OLD HAITIAN SLAVE SONG

CONTENTS

AUTHOR'S NOTE

EACH YEAR, on the island of Hispaniola, tens of thousands of Haitians cross into the Dominican Republic to work as cane cutters. These Haitians, or "Congos," as they are called on the other side of the border, bring their wives and children with them, and what awaits them all, without exception, is a life of untold privation and misery in working conditions patterned after the cruelest slave regimes.

Under these circumstances, which almost always last until the end of their days, the workers have no recourse but to cling to their religious beliefs—to the images of the gods, called "mysteries" or "loas," that they bring with them from Haiti. They group into "Societés" and gradually organize the Gagá: a form of worship, a festival, a hermetic and dedicated guild that few can penetrate. A prestigious Voudon priest assumes the position of "master" of the Gagá and spiritual leader of the flock, in which prominent roles are played by "elders," who are the highest-ranking men, and "queens," who are the most fearless women. Their most important festival takes place during Holy Week and centers on a hallucinatory excursion or pilgrimage through the fields that surround the sugar mill. This journey, marked by many ritual stopping points, lasts for three days and ends on Easter Sunday. Sometimes the Gagá travels great distances, through much of the countryside, and frequently crosses paths with another Gagá. The encounter can be absolutely cordial or extremely bloody, depending on the unpredictable mood of the "gods."

This novel narrates real events that occurred a few years ago in La Romana. It is a story of love, hatred, and death involving a "houngan," or Voudon priest, and a "mambo," or Voudon priestess, a woman who was very well known and respected in the region. The names of people and some places have been changed to protect certain informants. Behind a case closed by the Dominican police as a simple "crime of passion" pulse the magic spells of a war that is still being waged.

THE RED OF HIS SHADOW

A s IF THE SUN had split in two above the country-side, a few husks of light scatter over the world and boiling cane juice spills unimpeded onto the batey. Never had so intense a fire burned on a Holy Thursday. Never. Not even in the Year of the Deaths, when rabid mongooses climbed into the cradles of the newborn and no spell or protection could chase them away.

Mistress Zulé has been looking at the sun for a long time, searching with staring eyes for the temporal cause of its fury. She is soon joined by Jérémie Candé, her most cherished bodyguard, and he squats down beside her, trying to look where she is looking.

"It's hot," says Zulé.

The dogs and children have run off to hiding places where they won't be tortured by the sun. But the men of the Gagá, those who display the untouchable dignity of elders, have remained outside in defiance of the heat, tying perfumed rows of handkerchiefs around their sweaty bodies, large colored handkerchiefs, all the handkerchiefs they can, while those women who are queens by right finish trimming the bows of their crowns and fan themselves in silence. Everything is ready, everything arranged. Later, when the heat moderates, the mistress will go with those closest to her to free the beings who live in the Palm, offer them their food, light for them the flame of proclamation, then carry it secretly back to the batey. Tonight they will celebrate and tomorrow they will leave without having slept, and the aroma of the food they will offer to those who make the promise, to those who sing loudly, to every person who endures too fierce a trance, is already floating in the air.

"You'll burn your eyes," says Jérémie, who cannot bear to see the way she looks at the oily sky, at the air confounded by light.

She does not tremble when she asks what she must:

"Have you heard anything about Similá Bolosse?"

Jérémie Candé is her oldest servant, her oldest initiate. He is still very young, almost as young as she is, but since the time of her coronation he has followed her as submissively as if a holy amarre had been put on him.

"We know he made the vow again," he replies. "He swore he'd kill you and yesterday he was bathing in blood."

Zulé closes her eyes and seems to see the villain's face. How many goats, she wonders, and how many guinea hens had their heads cut off so that the bokor's huge body could be submerged in the tide of blood? Similá knows all too well that only in this way will his vow take on flesh; only in this way will he avoid having to resort to an ambush. Because he wants to kill her face-to-face; he wants to drown her, with his own hands, in the turbulent shallows of the river they call the Brujuelas.

"He can make all the vows he wants," she says. "We'll see who's stronger."

Sweet, soft sounds begin to be heard all around the batey. The queens are testing the echoes of their conch shells. Zulé listens and smiles, and then tilts back her black, burning head.

"It's hot," she repeats. "Go tell the men to test the bamboos."

No one in the batey can understand why the mistress has chosen to leave her house and sit outside on the ground in the middle of the day, at the mercy of the brutally hot scrub. Some speculate that she is thinking about the battle and perhaps at the last minute will take the advice of her elders and decide to travel along another route to avoid the fight. But Zulé is the mistress and no mistress ever listens to the advice of the men who are considered her counselors.

"The tatúas have to be tested too," she says quietly. "Everything has to be tested."

He didn't sleep the night before. How could he sleep knowing that Similá was splashing in an enormous dark lake of congealing blood; deep black blood that would fill him with enough strength to cut to pieces the woman in command. In the morning he learned that Zulé had not slept either. No one told him. No one spied on her. But everyone saw in her face the reddened marks of the flame, the cut lips, the wild eyes she had when a mystery mounted her for a long time, many times, and with a good deal of rancor.

"Do you want some rum?"

She refuses, shaking her head slowly, and he begins to walk toward the shacks. In a little while Zulé's Gagá is going to wake to the sweet sound of the tamboras. The children will abandon their shaded holes, the dogs will approach with dark tongues lolling, and the president of the Societé will give the order for the queens and elders to go to their huts and adorn themselves in peace. At the same time, but far away, in the Colonia Tumba batey, the terrible tentacles of Similá's Gagá will begin to stir, summoned by the vibrant sound of the fututos. They will alert the members who have moved away without permission, and still it will be necessary to plead for a little order before the machete of the Grand Bois is raised, gleaming for war.

"What did she say to you?"

Somebody stops Jérémie Candé, taking hold of his arm. It is Papa Luc, and he is trembling, but it's no secret to anyone there that his fear is not for himself, his own life. His fear is for the light that still glimmers in the terrible blankness of his eyes. His fear is for Zulé.

"Your daughter's very stubborn," Jérémie answers. "She doesn't want to listen."

Papa Luc's hands are long and badly cracked, as if they had been crushed in an assassin's fist. Contact with his fingers scrapes the flesh like sandpaper, and his fingernails stink of rotting fruit.

"They bathed Similá in blood," the old man says in the stumbling voice of his only sorrow.

The other man bends his head. Hiding it from him has been useless: Papa Luc always hears whatever he wants to hear, no matter where the words are said.

"We'll take care of her," Jérémie promises, trying to free his arm from the grim judgment of those fingers.

"Everybody in the Societé knew, everybody except this poor old man," and he turns his face away as if something suddenly repelled him.

Jérémie Candé is pained by the houngan's grimace, just as he is pained by the mannish obstinacy of Zulé, alone out there, broiling under that hellish sun.

"Now we don't have time to put a better amarre on him," the old man laments.

Time is what they've never had, Jérémie thinks calmly. And the houngan knows it very well, as do the rest of the elders. Or were they planning to put a death amarre on a man like Similá? He was powerful, he often crossed the border into Haiti to buy his dead in Locarre, in Hato del Curo, in Castilleur. He'd return to his batey fortified, bringing new powers for his pouch, ready to establish all the alliances he wanted.

"What can we do now?" the old man insists, his gray, vengeful eyeteeth showing at the corners of his mouth.

Jérémie Candé is very young. He has always been respectful of the old and an enemy of confrontations. But at this unusual moment it doesn't trouble him to say what he thinks:

"What we're going to do is cut off his balls," he says sharply. "Cut them off, Papa, with these hands."

T HEY NEVER PUT an amarre on Zulé's Gagá. The Gagá was never broken. Three or four years earlier it would set out like a whirlwind on Good Friday and return intact on Easter Sunday, more weighted down with offerings than weariness. This is how it had been for a long time, with no need for exchanges or alliances.

Zulé Revé, the Gagá's absolute mistress, had come to Colonia Engracia when she was still a shy, awkward girl frightened of other people's voices. She had been born in Grosse Roche and reared in a settlement at the foot of Mayombe Hill, beside the same river that carried away almost every member of her family, one after the other. Her two brothers had drowned there, playing recklessly in the swollen river; her mother drowned when she tried to rescue some hens; her grandmother, a taciturn, half-blind mambo, disappeared when she took a wrong turn and did nothing to save herself. And, finally, her father's second wife slipped while she was bathing, caught off guard by a rush of water that returned her three days later, her skin green, her neck broken, her body covered with snails.

Luc Revé, who was already a houngan, understood that the amarre was in the water, and to loosen amarres deep in the river a fire was needed that he could not light even with all the mysteries on his side. That's why he decided to emigrate, to take his daughter and cross the border and cut sugar cane in the Dominican Republic. His brother, Jean-Claude Revé, lived there, and his sister-in-law, who was not a Haitian but scarcely seemed anything else. They both had sent a message saying he should escape that land of misfortune and save the girl. After all, he had cut cane as a young man, on a plantation in Dajabón. He knew the trade and all its tricks, he knew how to cringe for the overseers and how to survive the merciless hell of the cane fields.

In those days the Colonia Engracia batey was a much more withdrawn and silent place; it had only one barracks to house the Congos, who were seasonal cutters; twelve wooden shacks that belonged to the "old-timers," which is what they called people who had lived in the Dominican Republic for a long time; fifteen or twenty huts to accommodate new families; and a few shelters without walls where migrant laborers, tramps, and dogs would huddle together late at night. Zulé was lucky. While her father had no choice but to sleep in the barracks, she was taken in by her uncle's family, into the same shack of mud and planks where her five cousins, all boys, welcomed her in befuddlement, wondering at her kinky bush of hair and the nocturnal enchantment of her strong white teeth.

Jean-Claude Revé's wife was a clairvoyant, patient Dominican who decided to marry the Haitian despite a rain of curses from her family that poured down on her for a long time afterward. All the cutters wanted a wife. All of them needed one. Haitian girls would frequently cross the border illegally and come to the bateys to see if anyone was interested in living with them. The Dominican girls, however, were like distant, scornful queens who looked down at the cutters from the height of their superiority, reluctant to join their improved flesh to the dusty blackness of those creatures in the cane fields.

Jean-Claude Revé was a fortunate man: Anacaona's love for him defied the beatings threatened by her father, the pitiless mockery of her best friends, and the unconfessable contempt of the Haitian women, who saw her come into their domain and swore they would put an amarre on her and all her hateful relatives. But Anacaona won them over one by one. She learned to say their words and cook their dishes, and when her first child was born and came out as black as Jean-Claude, people eventually forgot where she had come from.

When Zulé arrived with her father, Anacaona was expecting her sixth male child and her belly was dangerously pointed, as if she had been impregnated by Guedé. Even so, she had the tub brought in full of water and put the girl inside. Zulé cried, she bit the hands that held her down and beat against the sides of that lake darkened by filth. Anacaona, who was close to term, paid no attention and went on bathing her and occasionally, to quiet her, sang in the intricate language of the cane cutters: *Osanyo, lamizé pa dous, agoé* (Osanyo, misery is not sweet, agoé). In the days that followed she taught Zulé how to cook on the portable stove and showed her the path she would take out to the fields to bring Papa Luc his lunch. Zulé wasn't a clever girl, she frequently caught cold, and she shed easy tears that she always swallowed alone, always in the underbrush, always naked.

Nude and bathed in tears—that was how they found her in

the plantain grove two days after Anacaona gave birth to an infant that was beautiful, pale, and dead. Zulé had embraced the idea that she would take care of the baby herself, and when the midwife came out to announce that he had strangled on the cord, she fled to open country, pulled off her dress, and gave herself over to an uncontrollable fit of crying that no one but her father could stop. The promise made to her then by Papa Luc would mark forever the course of both their lives. He promised to take her to Coridón's Gagá to watch their preparations. And she instantly grew calm.

The Colonia Azote batey lay a little to the north, on the outskirts of Yerba Buena, and every year, in the month of February, the inhabitants of Colonia Engracia arranged to travel there and attend the rehearsals of the most remarkable Gagá in the region. Papa Coridón was a peaceable, accommodating man who allowed outsiders to gather in his domain and watch the practice sessions as long as they brought an offering to help along the toque. And so Zulé's father bought a bottle of rum for the occasion, and at dusk on Saturday, although he had just come back exhausted from the fields, he went out to the road with his daughter to catch a ride that would take them to the celebration. Anacaona had combed the girl's hair for the first time in many days, and Uncle Jean-Claude gave her a red handkerchief to tie around her neck. At eight o'clock, when they climbed down from the truck near Azote, they could already hear the incomplete roar of the bamboos and Zulé, deeply moved and chastened, began to walk toward the center of the batey.

Coridón was no taller than a boy, and he dressed in short pants and always wore a blue baseball cap with the visor over his left ear. Only his powerful arms and stonecutter's hands testified to his being a man in his forties who had seen something of the world, and only at the back of his fiery eyes could one detect the soul of a tough, pugnacious master. Those were the eyes that looked, still incredulous, into the confused eyes of the girl Zulé. She moved forward to see the dancing more closely, breaking through the circle of spectators, and one of the Gagá's guards came over and ordered her back. Zulé not only refused but walked directly to the spot where at that very moment an eternal group of queens was singing an old, seditious song:

Atibô Legbá, l'uvri bayé pu mwê, agoé!
Papa-Legbá, l'uvri bayè pu mwê,
Pu mwê pasé.

(Atibo Legbá, open the gate for me!
Papa-Legbá, open the gate
so I can go in.)

Zulé stopped just in front of the chorus and began to sway without moving her feet, without bending her head, without spreading her arms. Papa Coridón took a cigarette from one of his elders and went straight to where the girl was standing. Then the queens darkened the tone of their songs and Papa Luc tried to step forward to rescue his daughter but the guards stopped him, and Zulé didn't even bother to look at him. Besides, it was too late: Coridón stood in front of her, puffing intently on his cigarette, looking at her as if he had finally found her after long years of searching. Zulé's expression did not change and she did not stop swaying, and Papa Coridón raised his hands and held her face as if he were going to kiss it. She shook herself free, tore off the handkerchief she wore around her neck, and with partially open lips waited for the assault by the houngan of Azote, who brought the lit end of the cigarette closer to her. The elders blew wildly on their whistles and people crowded together to witness this encounter that the night promised to produce. Master Coridón pushed hard until the reddened ash was extinguished on Zulé's throat. She remained standing but he dropped like lead, rolled in the dust, twisted and turned as he gasped for breath, mute and choking on a pellet of terror. They came to his aid with the magic spray of aguardiente, they rubbed his crazed head, and all of them lifted him until he finally vomited up the howl directed at the most inflamed petrós of the night. When Papa Luc came to get his daughter, one of the elders said that Coridón wanted to talk to him. Zulé sat under a tree where some of the queens were comforting her, and he felt something resembling fear and something resembling pride when he observed the delicate appearance of the girl who had been tested by fire. Papa Coridón had recovered his conciliatory tone, and after greeting Luc Revé, he jammed the blue cap, blackened by the dirt, back on his head. In the light of the kerosene lamp, his rag-doll legs looked smaller and the brute strength of his arms more out of place. He handed a bottle of rum to Papa Luc and waited until he had swallowed the first mouthful before making the request that came from his very soul:

"You have to promise that girl."

Papa Luc continued drinking as if he hadn't heard him. And when he finally detached himself from the bottle, he directed a respectful and melancholy glance at the master of the Gagá:

"She's very young. She's only twelve."

"Twelve years that are worth a thousand," said Coridón, adopting an air close to resignation.

Not another word was said. Papa Luc felt ill at ease, and his most legitimate recourse was to take refuge in the bottle and lift it to his mouth over and over again until the First Queen, with the self-confident manner of an undisputed leader, came into the house and returned the girl to him. Papa Luc did not fail to notice the charged look that passed between them: Zulé looked at Coridón and Coridón looked at her as if they were sworn to each other.

By midnight they were back in Colonia Engracia, and Papa Luc went straight to Jean-Claude's house to drop off the girl. Anacaona was not asleep yet, and she came out to greet them, her eyes radiant.

"They say you're going to promise your daughter . . ."

It was true: news traveled fast. Each day he spent in the batey, Papa Luc learned something different. And that night he had learned that great secrets did not exist in the lives of men, only small snares waiting at each step, the bait lying right there on the ground.

"Did you like the Gagá, Zulé my girl?"

She asked the question with the gentle irony of proven love. Anacaona was happy for Zulé, happy she would be promised to a Gagá as prestigious as Coridón's. Papa Luc bent down and kissed his daughter, who went into the house rubbing her eyes as if she were just waking up. He walked to the barracks to sleep for three or four hours. A handful of cane cutters rested on Sunday, but the majority preferred to work seven days and make the most of the season before the Dead Time came. At four in the morning the overseer rang the bell, and within fifteen minutes the men were in the truck that would take them to the fields. It had been this way for a long time, and now that his daughter would be promised to the most warlike Gagá in the country, he had no reason to change.

Papa Luc was awake all that night and couldn't close his eyes on the next. On the third day, when he had just begun hacking the

stalks, he thought he saw a white rabbit in the canebrake. It occurred to him that the animal wouldn't last very long with all the
starving snakes hiding under the cane debris that littered the
ground. But at midday he saw other rabbits hopping on the trash,
and by nightfall the whole field was a swarm of animals chasing
after their prey. He mentioned it to another cutter, a boy from
Jacmel, who opened his eyes wide and told the others. They
bound Luc Revé and dragged him back to the barracks, rigid and
green with convulsions. It could have been malaria or it might
have been dengue. Whatever the fever was, it carried him forward, it carried him far, it cooked him slowly under the red brilliance of eyes that only could be the ferocious eyes of a rabbit.

A little before midnight two men went to Jean-Claude's
wooden shack to tell him his brother was dying. Anacaona woke
Zulé, who was in a deep sleep, and they walked together to the
barracks, where they found a kind of gasping corpse surrounded
by a chorus of agitated cutters who were tossing buckets of cold
water on Luc Revé and spraying rum at him.

"A snake must have bitten him," said Jean-Claude, who came
rushing in. "Zulé, you look for the bite."

She obeyed, convinced it was perhaps the last favor she would
do for her father. They brought lanterns and shined the light on
him front and back, but found nothing. When they held the light
to his face, Papa Luc moaned and looked for the girl who was the
apple of his eye.

"You have to promise yourself next month," he told her.
"Whatever happens you go there and promise yourself for me."

Zulé smiled and placed her warm hand on his burning forehead: of course she would promise herself, she said.

"I think it's the best thing," her father managed to say before
he sank into the stupor of a cure by touch.

In a short while the fever had gone down, and the entire family left the barracks certain that Luc Revé would be healed. It was just a matter of giving him good food, and Anacaona hurried to cook a cornmeal porridge with noodles that she sent over with her husband. On Wednesday Papa Luc had been dying, but by Saturday he had recovered sufficiently to take his daughter to the rehearsals of Coridón's Gagá for a second time. The master received him affectionately and asked how he was feeling. He knew very well that Zulé's father had been sick and once again Luc Revé marveled at how quickly news flew under the elemental sky of the bateys. Papa Coridón came straight to the point: the festival was just a few weeks away. After the ceremony on Holy Thursday, they would rest until dawn of Good Friday and then travel to the bateys of Mata Palacio, Guayabo Dulce, and Los Chicharrones. They weren't going to visit Hato Mayor because the Town Council always refused to let them in. But he wanted Zulé to go on the pilgrimage with them and be welcomed the right way in Colonia Engracia. She should see the bateys on this side of San Pedro and be presented to the houngan Papa Señor, a famous Dominican who lived on the banks of the Macorís.

"I want your daughter to see the world," he concluded, staring at Papa Luc.

It had all been said. From then on, Saturday after Saturday, Luc Revé traveled with his daughter to Yerba Buena so the girl could learn the songs and practice the dances and be taught the duties of the one being promised, which were many and very subtle. The commitment lasted seven years, and during that time she would receive protection from the Gagá in exchange for difficult tests of her fidelity.

On one of those nights, when there was still a week to go before her promising ceremony, Zulé did not travel back to Colonia

Engracia with her father. Papa Luc stopped by his brother's wooden house to tell Anacaona not to expect the girl.

"She stayed there, she has to do a retreat," he said, and his sister-in-law looked at him with a certain distrust and sorrow.

"Well, you shouldn't have left her. She's very young."

"I know that," he replied. "But what can I do, even you encouraged her to make the promise."

"Promising is one thing," Anacaona snapped. "Leaving her there with that pack of Congos is something else again."

She had forgotten where the girl came from, and Luc Revé, and her husband. Or Anacaona the Dominican had just remembered her own origins. For a long time it had not even passed through her mind that she had been born in Las Galeras, beside the sea, far from almost everything, and particularly far from Haiti.

"We don't bite, even if we are Congos," he said, choking back a sarcastic little laugh.

She tried to put things right and only made matters worse. But Papa Luc was not about to take offense at what was really a trifle, and he changed the subject. He asked for Jean-Claude, who was asleep, and then he waved good-bye and disappeared into the night on his way to the barracks of his misfortunes.

On Holy Wednesday, the eve of the ceremonial Raising of the girl, Luc Revé came back early from the fields. His brother was waiting for him with the gift of a tub of water and clean clothes, and Anacaona, excited by the trip, agreed to lend him her perfumed soap. She too was going to wear her finest: a ruffled blouse, the orange skirt she had inherited from one of her sisters, and the chain necklace she wore for parties.

"You'd better dress fast," she told her brother-in-law. "The truck's ready to leave."

A good part of the Colonia Engracia batey crowded into the truck. For the whole ride Jean-Claude kept his arms around his wife so the eager cutters couldn't take advantage of the pushing and shoving, while his brother Luc, who didn't take his eyes off them, promised himself that when the harvest was over he would choose one of those women who came across from Haiti, and set up his own little shack. The mere thought of it lit up his life, and wearing the tranquil expression of his plans, he saw in the distance the first huts of Colonia Azote, where the great Gagá of Coridón, frenzied and tumultuous, was about to explode.

H ONORÉ BABIOLE IS HERE."
Before he even finishes speaking, Mistress Zulé, who has spent a long time squatting under the Bower, turns abruptly and looks into his eyes as if demanding one more word.

"He asked to see you right away."

She gestures with her head and orders her elders to continue placing decorations on the blond tufts of royal palm. This year the Engracia Bower has to be the most extravagant, the most perfect and adorned, in the Dominican Republic.

"Did he go to Boca Chica?"

She asks the question in a quiet voice, almost reluctantly. No one could tell there is a gnawing in her soul to know the answer. No one except Jérémie Candé.

"He went there and checked the route. He says Similá plans to go there."

Zulé closes her eyes and Jérémie torments himself in vain. He cannot console her, he can only squeeze his lids shut too and despise everything he is hearing, especially the deceit in his own voice.

"Well, let him go," she explodes. "Who'll carry the pouch?"

The burning midday heat has eased. But from the dry earth a heavy mist rises that smells, as always, of cassava, parched dung, and dead bagasse.

"Tarzán Similá, the master's son, will carry it."

He was going to add something about the weapons, but he restrains himself. You have to give Zulé specific answers as she asks for them. Otherwise she rears back and bites like a carelessly tied iguana.

"They'll bring their machetes, won't they?"

"They prepared clubs," Jérémie takes advantage of the opportunity. "And they'll carry knives."

Honoré Babiole doesn't live in the Colonia Engracia batey. He cuts cane at another mill, but three years ago he promised himself to Zulé's Gagá, and for the past two years it has been his job to learn the route that Similá's Gagá will follow. His information has never been wrong. Honoré has blood kin in the Colonia Tumba batey. He is a friend of friends of the elders, and his brother, Truman Babiole, is sworn there.

"Similá's hungry for a fight," says Jérémie, and he gulps for air as if he had just come out of the water.

"Tell me the rest . . ."

They start to walk toward the shacks, and on the way Zulé begins to sniff the breeze, she cranes her neck and moves her head from side to side, like an animal coming out of its lair.

"He'll bring pistols. Somebody tipped off Honoré."

She stops abruptly. Coridón had taught her that Gagá wars can be very good. Good when you make an alliance and the Societé fattens like a majá snake in the shade and the men are barely bruised by an unlucky stone. But who ever heard of firearms in Gagá battles? It needed Similá Bolosse with his evil tonton macoute ways for things in the Dominican Republic to stop being what they had been.

"He's going to shoot us with bullets," Jérémie Candé adds. "Wherever he catches us, he'll shoot us."

At moments like this Zulé feels the pain of her old teacher's absence. Coridón could have decided, with no fear of making a mistake, if she is the one who has to give in and change her route, or if she ought to confront Similá Bolosse. But her godfather and guide died several years ago during his chaotic ride through a dangerous trance that left him without a soul and no chance to say good-bye.

"Your father's with Honoré," says Jérémie when they reach the house. "Go in and listen to them."

With anyone but Jérémie Candé she would have punished the insolence of suggesting things to her. But this is a day too heavy with bad omens and her thoughts are too far away. Papa Luc is inside, pouring rum into a little aluminum cup, and beside him is the unfathomable Honoré Babiole, who looks at her with compassion.

"The man's carrying pistols," her father blurts out as soon as he sees her come in. "The party's over."

Honoré is older and craftier. And he knows right away she won't be persuaded so easily.

"You should change the route your people take," he says. "If they run into Similá there'll be a lot of blood, there'll be deaths and many people wounded. And the devil will carry off anyone left to tell the tale."

"But you won't find Similá Bolosse with the dead," says an

agitated Papa Luc, "and you won't find him with the wounded or the ones who go to jail. He'll bury everybody, including you, girl."

As soon as she sits down Zulé breaks into a sweat, releasing the suffocating heat she has brought in with her from outside. She breathes with her mouth open, and her chest rises and falls with the whistling of a distant animal.

"The Town Council won't let you in San Pedro, and they won't let you in Hato Mayor," says Honoré. "I think they smell something. They'll let you tear yourselves to pieces in the fields and then they'll round you up like cattle."

"Everybody except Similá," her father insists.

In the melancholy mists of her mind she searches for the war-like image of the man who was so humbled when she first met him. It happened one March when Anacaona woke her earlier than usual to say that a bokor who had just come from Haiti was in the batey. Zulé greeted him uneasily because he came from Paredón, a village on the shores of Peligre Lake, and she remembered that Coridón once warned her that the bokors from this region were known as the most implacable and powerful along the entire border. Similá Bolosse, trying to swallow more rum than his mouth could hold, told her part of the truth that morning: he had fled his village on the same day the big boss fell in Port-au-Prince, when the mobs who stoned to death the boss of the ton-ton macoutes swore they'd tear the bokor apart too. He hid in a nearby plantain grove and then escaped to the countryside where he survived for ten days eating roots and scorpion tails. When he finally crossed into the Dominican Republic, he was a ghost riddled with the transparent pockmarks of savanna disease. Later he learned that his temple had been destroyed, his altars sent on to a better life, and his four dogs killed in the cruelest, most painful way. Still, he was grateful for the life he still had between his chest and his back. Bull-Trois-Graines, the wild beast with three balls, had protected him then and would protect him always, always, always . . .

"We go at five in the morning," Zulé says, returning to the present. "We go the way we're supposed to go."

Her voice sounds serene and cool, so steady it doesn't seem to come from her afflicted throat that flutters like a bird.

"The way we're supposed to go, Mistress? They'll tear us to pieces."

Luc Revé's voice also sounds deliberate, and his words come out anointed with the sorrowful cadence of one who knows he will never say them again.

"I thought the harm put on me in the river at Mayombe had stayed in the river. That's what I thought, but now I see that they'll kill my only daughter and throw her in too. It's been decreed that all the women in this line will meet their end in water."

Honoré Babiole, more subtle than Zulé's father, tries one last time.

"Similá's a viper," he says very quietly. "He swore he'd kill you face-to-face, but he'll attack you anywhere he can. Yesterday he bathed in the blood of a hundred goats whose throats were cut so that Lokó Siñaña would clear the way for him. Tell me, Mistress Zulé, what will you say afterwards to the dead men's families?"

She extends her arm and takes the aluminum cup and what remains of the rum from her father's hand. Luc Revé looks at her with the well-washed eyes of a man already contemplating a corpse.

"We go at five," Zulé repeats. "I'm going, Jérémie's coming too. I don't know who else will want to come with me."

The question remains floating for a few moments over their heads. It will soon grow dark and she will have to adorn herself for the Raising of the Chair, the ceremony that has always moved her the most. But before that she'll have to feed the Central Post of the Bower. Jérémie Candé will be in charge of cutting the casabe and stripping the ears of corn, and Christianá Dubois, the War Queen, will choose the pieces of coconut and fill the little bags with peanuts. When everything is ready, Zulé will crouch down and dig the hole where the offerings are buried: she'll open it with her hands, fertilize it with a sprig of basil, and fill it with provisions. Finally, she'll draw on the ground, with the pure ash of days, the intricate signs of the Vevé. All so that the loas will know, so that the mysteries are not agitated, so that the world comes to see that her fear is not greater than her heart.

"I want you to pray tonight," she tells her father.

Luc Revé has not prayed in the Gagá for many years. He used to, when the Societé was very small and nobody in the batey knew the words. But then competent people arrived who used the traditional tone for murmuring protections, and without thinking too much about it he gave up his place to them. Tonight he will pray again beside the mistress. He will raise his voice at the moment she sprinkles holy water on the clothing of all her elders, on crowns and banners, on staffs and pouches, and on the vibrating skins of tamboras whose breathing can almost be heard.

"Now I'm going to get dressed."

The two men stand and Honoré Babiole looks at her solemnly. But her father stares at the ground, as if he were about to cast a spell to make the earth open at his feet. Zulé sees him trembling from head to foot.

"Old man, you must be cold," she says, making the superhuman effort that tenderness has always cost her. "Doesn't your wife give you anything to eat?"

As for the rest, there is no turning back. When they leave the house Papa Luc and Honoré Babiole talk briefly with the members of the Societé who have been gathering outside. It is for Zulé's father, as First Elder, to rouse the group. For that reason alone, in order not to disappoint anyone, he clears his throat, stands on a crate, and shouts his words with the all-powerful voice of misfortune:

"Similá Bolosse will be looking for a fight and he's carrying pistols. We go at five sharp, and whoever wants to come will show what kind of balls he has."

S HORTLY AFTER the coronation of Zulé the great
drought began. More than a year had gone by since the
night of Holy Thursday when she was promised to Coridón's
Gagá, and in that time she had become a precocious, instinctive
mambo whom people came to consult from places as far away as
Isla Saona and Cabo Cabrón.

As they raised her in the Chair and led her to the Bower, Zulé
fell into a trance that lasted until Easter Sunday. Following the
expressed desire of Papa Coridón, she accompanied them on the
pilgrimage they began at dawn on Good Friday, which took them
first to the Colonia Engracia batey, where they were welcomed by
a frenzied toque that lasted all afternoon. Then they continued
south so that Zulé could see the bateys on this side of San Pedro.
Finally, Coridón himself led her to the banks of the Macorís in order to present her to Papa Señor, the famous Dominican houngan
who prophesied a great and fortunate future for the girl.

They returned to Yerba Buena on the night of Easter Sunday, with full collection boxes and so many offerings that a month later they were still eating guinea hens given to them on the sugar plantations. Although the rehearsals for the Gagá were over and the Societé had returned to more tranquil days, Zulé continued to visit the Colonia Azote to learn from Coridón the law of amarres and protections ("You put an amarre on a man to break his soul, to hurt him, to kill him; or you protect him so that nobody breaks him, nobody hurts him, nobody kills him"); the law for laying down a spell-pot ("Look at the cauldron: everything is together, nothing is mixed up, the bones of Christians on one side, the innards of the animal on the other, only with order does your pot boil with powers, listen carefully, Zulé my girl, your greatest powers"); and the very difficult law of caring for the dead ("Wash the corpse, cut away the innards that still tie him to this world, and beat him, beat him hard so he howls like a baby, a dead man is a baby, Zulé, never forget it"). But during that time nothing—not her novice's arts, the weeping diligence of her father, the belated intervention of Coridón himself—nothing could prevent Uncle Jean-Claude from dying a black death.

On other occasions he had been stung by wasps in the cane fields and had to be taken back to his hut, his body swollen and his tongue twisted by the venomous buzzing of his own blood. Anacaona would be waiting with the remedy, and in a few hours he'd begin to recover the gift of speech with a drunkard's slobbering moans and the bulging eyes of one who has seen the smoking phallus of death. Unlike the other cane cutters, who suffered only a few painful welts from wasp stings, Jean-Claude would be left with suppurating chancres as virulent as smallpox and as deep as a bullet wound. This last time, however, the wasp stung him in a vein in his neck, and he only had time to stagger back to his house, collapse in front of his children, and die with fetid roars that Anacaona still heard in dreams months after he was buried.

Zulé, who was in the house when they brought back Jean-Claude, prepared desperate compresses and sprinkled him with holy water. Then she gave him a rag to suck that she had soaked in the potion used for snakebite. But nothing worked. Anacaona, at the age of twenty-three, was left alone to care for five boys and a clairvoyant niece who rescued her from tragedy with a happy solution:

"Marry my father."

The widow paused in her grieving for a moment, smiled at Zulé with a vague shadow of sadness, and acknowledged to herself that this was perhaps the only sensible idea of all those that had circled round her in recent days. Luc Revé was considerably older than his dead brother, and therefore considerably older than Anacaona, but he was a willing worker, and in her wretched state as the widow of a Haitian cane cutter with five boys as black as their father, she couldn't even consider the possibility of returning to her hometown of Las Galeras. She could, of course, choose one of the younger Haitians from the barracks. Any of them would have been more than honored to live with a good-looking mulatta who had her own house. But there was no reason to run the risk of putting up with a man who might turn out to be a drinker or a gambler, or what was even worse and more common among the single cutters, who might have a hernia and bad seed. And so one Monday night, when Papa Luc pretended to be paying his daughter a long visit, Anacaona heard him ask if he could sleep there. She said yes, but the truth is that nobody in the house slept that night except the two youngest orphans. Zulé's father had been without a woman for more than a year, and the widow herself had grown accustomed to Jean-Claude's enthusiastic frequency. They undressed without shame and in a frenzy fell into the rickety double bed that the deceased had left free and that didn't even survive the first assault. Not until it collapsed and they heard the giggles of Zulé and the older boys did Anacaona remember they were not alone. With great serenity she moved away from her new husband and lit a lantern, and with the same presence of mind began to scold the children. Zulé, in the meantime, observed the unusual sight of her aunt's nakedness and the delayed tremor that made her breasts quiver.

"I want to watch," Zulé said, barely disguising the command in her words.

Anacaona smiled and went back to the devastated bed where Luc Revé received her with his passion intact. They made love several times in the shifting ruins of the bed, and at daybreak, when the overseer began to ring the bell for the men to come out of the barracks, she got up to prepare coffee. She was still naked, and Zulé stayed at her side, looking at her sweaty belly and the slow drizzle that ran down her thighs.

"Now you'll let me live with Coridón."

Anacaona did not turn her head or say a word, but for a moment she stood still and then returned to the rubble of her bed, carrying the steaming pitcher of coffee. The clanging bell, which the overseer continued to ring outside, did not alarm Papa Luc very much, and he made a final effort to take control of his new wife's slippery belly.

"It's late," she said, handing him his work shirt, his tattered trousers, and a red handkerchief that she tried to tie around his head while he was licking her breasts.

Luc Revé left the house and joined the group of cutters leaving then for the fields. Anacaona and Zulé watched him through a crack and listened to the jokes they made about his move. Papa

Luc remained silent, filled with the proud contentment that victories with a woman can bring.

At lunchtime, Zulé, as she always did, prepared the plate with two pieces of cassava and a boiled plantain, but Anacaona stopped her at the door: now it was her job to carry it. She added a piece of casabe and began to walk along the dusty path, treeless and airless under the agonizing flame of the sun. Other women, and some of the children who took food to their fathers, walked with her, but when they finally reached the cane fields, the eyes of all the cutters rested only on her, on her satisfied face and perfect submissiveness as she handed him his plate.

Papa Luc endured another torrent of jokes. He swallowed all the cassava in two huge mouthfuls and took his time chewing the plantain, and before tasting the casabe he looked at his wife, his eyes brimming with gratitude: the additional food, more than a wedding gift, was a small recompense for the triumphs of the previous night; an undeniable sign that in the difficult contest of the flesh, he had won her over. Anacaona sat beside him on the stinging surface of the cane debris and looked out at the flat horizon.

"Those bastards are going to burn the cane," Luc Revé said suddenly, referring to the men from the mill.

She knew what burned cane meant: more work and less pay, because the piles of cane lost weight. She had already suffered through it in the flesh of her dead husband, who would come home with singed clothes and labored breathing. And many days after the milling was over, when the nightmare of the Dead Time began, Jean-Claude was still sweating the dangerous dark ink of the ash left embedded in his skin.

"The burning killed Jean-Claude," she said in a quiet voice.

He had been so preoccupied with the conquest of his new wife that Papa Luc had not thought again about his dead brother. He remembered little of their childhood, but one of the few things he did recall were poultices on the nights Jean-Claude couldn't catch his breath, the unbearable wailing of a baby on whom every ailment vented its rage.

"A lot of things killed Jean-Claude," he said. "Damp wind killed him, chicken feathers killed him, a woman's kisses killed him. He always sneezed after he fucked . . . Didn't he with you?"

Anacaona gave him a quick, rancorous look, and at that moment the overseer began to clap his hands and blow the whistle for the men to go back to work. Papa Luc gave her a farewell pinch on the buttock, and she picked up the empty plate without looking at him and without complaining. Before she went back the way she had come, she raised her hands to her head as if she had just remembered something.

"Your daughter Zulé says she's going to live with Coridón."

Luc Revé's face contorted and he took a step back.

"Coridón has a wife," he replied.

Anacaona hesitated, and her husband picked up his machete to start cutting again.

"Coridón's wife is the one who came for her."

At three in the afternoon the entire cane field would fall into a hallucinatory trance; it turned into a gigantic oven where dust from the bagasse and delayed embers from the burning cane floated; it became a nameless place that reminded everyone of hell.

"She isn't thirteen yet," Luc Revé insisted. He didn't want any trouble with Coridón.

That night, when he returned to the house, Zulé was still there. As were Master Coridón and his wife, a toothless, plump mulatta named María Caracoles, who was half Dominican and half Haitian and as affable and smiling as a simpleminded girl.

From time to time she caressed the kinky hair of Papa Luc's only daughter and kissed her cheeks.

"I came for her," Coridón said simply.

Luc Revé was worn out. His nocturnal battles and work in the cane fields had plunged him into the exhaustion of a dying animal. Anacaona removed the machete from his hands, took off his hat, and untied the red handkerchief he wore around his head.

"We'll crown her when the harvest's over," Coridón added. "We're making an alliance with Prévilé's Gagá."

Papa Luc thought that the dizzying ascension of his daughter was unlike anything ever seen in any Societé. He sought out the knowing eyes of Zulé, who at that moment was kissing Coridón's wife on the lips.

"What do you say, girl?"

She moved away slowly from her godfather's wife and faced her father with eyes like glass:

"I say yes, I want to be a queen."

Anacaona began to pack up Zulé's tattered clothing, and Papa Luc glanced at her, looking for support he couldn't find even in his own bones.

"Let her go," Anacaona advised. "Let her be."

The three of them left: Coridón, his plump wife, and the future queen who carried in her hands the haphazard bundle of her few belongings. Luc Revé thought everything would be all right if Anacaona had let her go, especially because he knew how full of visions and suspicions this wife of his was. That night he didn't have the heart for more battles. He caressed her indomitable breasts, licked her back for a while, and slept like a baby in the simple shade of that artful matron who lay for a time with her eyes opened wide. She too was exhausted, and when the harsh bell sounded at daybreak, she woke as unwillingly as she had fallen asleep. It seemed unbelievable that she had ever been a widow, because everything was falling into the commonplace routine of her misery: the weak coffee at dawn, the rhythmic braying from the bed, the figure of the cane cutter leaving for the fields, and then, at midday, the path martyrized by the sun for so many years, the warm plate of food for lunch, and the sting of the bagasse always sticking to her skin, always in her eyes, always crackling under her feet.

Several months later Zulé came to visit them. She was accompanied by María Caracoles and brought Coridón's present of two chickens, which Anacaona cooked that same day for lunch. It was María Caracoles, and not Papa Luc's daughter, who spoke of the girl's progress: her name was becoming important in the area, and it was common now for people to come from Hato Mayor and even El Seibo to consult with her. Only a week ago they had all been stunned when a Dominican from San Rafael del Yuma, a clean, well-to-do man, had come to beg the little Haitian from Engracia to put an amarre on the woman of his heart.

When Papa Luc returned that night he displayed great excitement at finding his daughter so grown, and he asked his wife for a glass of rum to wash down his happiness. María Caracoles told him, word for word, the same thing she had told Anacaona. But she also gave him a brief and very confidential message from Coridón, a few words that she whispered in his ear and didn't want anyone else to hear. Zulé contemplated them all as if she were in another world, and blushed when she informed them she would be crowned in thirty days with a great toque festival on the outskirts of Mandinga.

"That's in Santo Domingo!" Anacaona exclaimed, astonished at their going so far away.

Coridón's wife nodded: that's where Prévilé's Gagá was: he

was the houngan who would sponsor Zulé's crowning. If they liked, they could come to Yerba Buena on the day of the crowning and then travel with the rest of the Societé to Mandinga. Papa Luc said he would think about it, and Anacaona took out the orange skirt and white ruffled blouse she had not worn since Zulé's Raising.

"We'll go," she said.

Several days later the harvest was over. That night the mill siren wailed to announce the start of the Dead Time, and once again people pretended they hadn't heard the devastating clang when the mill stopped grinding, or the sickening buzz of the silence that would last well into the month of October. This was when the batey slumbered in the torpor of the worst heat, and the men scattered to look for work. The year before, Papa Luc had chopped weeds in gardens in the vicinity of La Romana, but this time Anacaona suggested he change direction and take advantage of the trip to Mandinga to stay near the capital.

On the eve of her crowning no one slept. Luc Revé spent the night helping his wife prepare tamales to bring to the celebration, and long before dawn they began walking to the highway to find a ride to the Colonia Azote batey. They arrived when the sun was fairly high, and a flurry of women carrying pots of food on their shoulders were shouting orders that nobody bothered to obey. María Caracoles came out to greet them and invited them to make themselves comfortable in her house until it was time to leave. Zulé was there too, watching the noisy preparations for her crowning as if she were hypnotized. Papa Luc approached her in silence and kissed her forehead, and Anacaona stood in front of her and modestly caressed both her cheeks.

"I can tell," she whispered.

Zulé did not take the trouble to pretend, but Anacaona clarified it for her anyway.

"I can tell you've tasted the flame."

Luc Revé, who was downing the day's first glass of rum, resigned himself to hearing their giggles. But he didn't ask anybody anything, not even Coridón, who came in just then with a skinny, slant-eyed boy as slippery and electric as an eel.

"This is my son," he announced as he slapped the boy hard on the back.

Anacaona immediately estimated that this son was more or less the same age as Zulé, and it was María Caracoles who told her that his mother was a Chinese chambermaid who worked on ships, and that Coridón once kept her on land with a blood amarre. The baby was born in Puerto Plata, his head misshapen because the Chinese chambermaid had bound her pregnant belly to hide it from the crew. A short while after giving birth she signed on another ship for a year and left the baby behind, and that was when Coridón, bearing his burden alone, decided to abandon the vagrant life of the docks and find work as a cane cutter. And so he came to the Colonia Azote batey with a little chameleon only a few months old whom he named Jérémie Candé. The boy grew up with the narrow eyes and straight hair of an Asian, but unfortunately he had inherited his father's twisted legs and hideous nose.

"He doesn't like anybody to tell him what to do," María Caracoles concluded. "Now the only person he listens to is Zulé."

To reach Mandinga they had to travel for several hours in an open truck that first took them down to San Pedro and then followed the burning heat of the coast road. The deadly lethargy of the drought was already rising from the earth, and Papa Luc, tormented by the sun's glare, covered his face and sighed, foreseeing disaster:

"It'll be hot."

In the days that followed the crowning the entire countryside was scorched. A plague of thirsty mongooses overran the bateys and destroyed the cane shoots. Protections were prepared, mysteries invoked, and hundreds of toques were held to placate the Baron of the Cemetery. People died of asphyxiation and they died above all of rabies. This lasted for six months, and like all the tragedies that have happened in the world, it was not until a good deal of time had passed that the survivors could give it a name: they called it the Year of the Deaths, and in its devastating, still-smoldering shadow, they tried to go on living.

THEY COME OUT of the barracks one by one, wrapped in their white sheets, as voracious and frightening as angry gods. They are the elders of the Colonia Engracia Gagá, their steps hesitant in feigned terror of the resurrection, their gestures hallucinatory with the high emotion of disturbing the hidden sleep of the next life. Zulé Revé, dressed completely in black in honor of Guedé Nibó, attentively searches out the eyes of her father, who marches at the head of the procession, and he immediately responds with a single lucid, virile glance that concedes all the triumph to her. Jérémie Candé smiles in spite of everything. Then he brings his lips close to Zulé's warm ear and whispers sweetly:

"You see, Mama, nobody will fail you."

The batey is in darkness, but in the cleared space the lady and mistress of the dawn, the sacred fire that inflames all the mysteries, is still burning.

"There's one who will fail me," she replies. "Papa Luc. I don't want him to come with us."

Jérémie Candé shaved his head the night before and has a number of cuts on his skull and some dried clots of blood clinging to his temples.

"How can you even think your father won't come? How can we leave him behind?"

The elders continue advancing, solemn in their winding sheets. The queens and the musicians also wander around the field, only waiting for a signal to make their way to the shack where the new clothes and the walking sticks, the pots for feeding the loas and the maracas that have been blessed, are all kept.

"You take care of keeping him here," she repeats. "Papa's old."

"I'm telling you he won't want to . . . Who ever saw a First Elder stay behind in the batey?"

"They'll see it today," Zulé finally spits out in the sacred voice of her approaching furies.

There is a pause so that everyone can dress, and in the meantime Zulé turns and walks to the sacred fire to make certain it will not be extinguished in her absence. Trapped inside the blue flames is the burning rod through which Ogún Ferraille, the old Baron of Iron, speaks and punishes.

"He won't want to stay," Jérémie Candé repeats and moves away before the mistress can lash out at him.

The truck that will take them on their pilgrimage looks very much like the one that took them to Mandinga on the day of her crowning. The years have passed, so many that Zulé doesn't dare to count them, but she still remembers the orange skirt with which Anacaona energized the entire celebration; she remembers the rolling eyes of Master Prévilé, the proudest houngan in the capital, when he tore off her blouse to beat her chest; and above all she remembers the awful rapture of Coridón, who writhed in ecstasy at her feet, asking Papa Legbá to burn him alive, roast him whole, send him an agony different from any past suffering.

"Coridón . . ."

She says it softly, staring at the flames as if trying to bury him again beneath the ashes of her memory. Then she is startled by a voice behind her that responds:

"Coridón's dead."

She recognizes the tone, the old huskiness. It is Honoré Babiole, who approaches her one more time, not to persuade her to change the original route but to teach her how she must fight when she finds herself face-to-face with Similá Bolosse, the wild boar.

"When you have death this close, it's not good to remember the dead you've loved. You know the dead pull hard at you."

She knows and has always feared it. Especially as a girl, when she bathed on the banks of the river and felt as if all the drowned people in her family came up from the bottom to suck at her.

"Don't summon them, Mistress Zulé, not Coridón, not anybody . . . You listen to what I'm telling you."

At last she stops staring at the fire and turns her head to look at her oldest confidant. He has dressed in the ceremonial clothing of an elder and she knows what that signifies: this time Honoré Babiole will travel with them, and the journey will mark the end of his mission as scout for Colonia Tumba. But even more serious is that this journey will probably mark the end of his life.

"I didn't tell anybody to sew those clothes for you."

"I know," says Honoré. "They belong to your father."

It's not that he lacks dignity. On the contrary, he has honorably risked his life bringing news from one place to the other, revealing the plans of the outsider who is trying to control all the Societés in the region. Honoré Babiole was the one who reported that Similá gets his money from Haiti, where the old macoute bosses have ordered him to infiltrate the bateys, guarantee a safe, permanent route for traveling north through the Dominican Republic, and maintain a beachhead in Boca Chica. And it was Honoré who discovered that Similá and his son Tarzán pick up boat shipments in Guayacanes, bundles wrapped in black nylon that they usually hide in Colonia Tumba and then take to Puerto Plata, where a schooner is always waiting for them.

"If I don't want my father to come," says Zulé, "then I don't want you either; you're even older."

Honoré smiles and points his finger at the flames of the bukán:

"Look at Ogún Ferraille's prick. Look how hard it is, and he's really old."

This is when Zulé laughs out loud for the first time in a very long while.

"You got your way, woman. Nobody backed down."

The musicians have begun to play near the truck, and Honoré Babiole tries a few dangerous leaps over the fire. She can't forget that this was the man who closed Coridón's eyes on the Holy Saturday when the houngan of Azote did not come back from the ecstasy of a trance. It was Honoré who comforted her with four good words: "You're grown up now," and he was the one who accompanied Zulé on her anguished, triumphant return to Colonia Engracia.

"Don't think about the dead," he tells her now. "Remember that the dead pull at the living."

Then his face grows somber and he looks at her across the flames: Zulé has to listen, she has to understand as well that it's not a question of letting themselves be slaughtered as if they were hogs. It's true they don't have pistols, but the men of Colonia Engracia have more than enough of what they need to cut off the balls of a poisonous viper like Similá Bolosse. He'll ask Zulé for only one thing: he'll ask her not to take part.

"You're asking the mistress not to take part in her Gagá?"

Honoré Babiole partially modifies what he has said:

"In the fight, Zulé. Stay out of the fight."

The dawn is overcast, and one doesn't need to know much about the law of the sky to predict that by noon the storm will break.

"Stay here with Papa Luc," she orders for the last time.

"Papa Luc won't stay behind either," Honoré replies. "He gave me his outfit because he's going in ordinary clothes. He's going as the lamé, he wants to carry the whip and clear your path, that's what he told me."

During Lent and until the end of Holy Week, the rainstorms in the region around Colonia Engracia smell irremediably of the sea. At times fish have come down with the rain, sardines of some kind that flop in the mud for a while and by the next day are rotting carrion, flooding every corner of the batey with their awful stink. The oldest laborers still remember the day when a hurricane stronger than most dropped the corpse of a small shark in the fields, an animal of steel that still clenched between its teeth the impossible neck of a bird.

"I don't think I'm the mistress anymore," Zulé murmurs sadly. "Today everybody's making decisions in my Gagá."

Honoré Babiole looks at the deep, dark storm clouds approaching slowly from the south.

"We'd better get started."

He escorts her to the truck, and on the way she begins to hum the music of the bamboos. Honoré watches her growing excitement, he watches her spread her arms and run toward the elders, who are blowing their whistles. The entire batey crowds onto the road to say good-bye to the leaders of the Gagá, but when the first lightning flashes, the musicians stop abruptly:

Loray grondé . . . grondéeeeeee

It is the voice of the mistress, which now seems to come from the depths of a cursed well. Nothing can stop them now, no amarre can bind them or frighten them, and the players, stirred by this signal from their mistress, resume the almost perverse rhythm of the song:

Loray grondé . . . Agau soti lâ Guinê!
Pwason volé,
syel-la se lanmé,
lanmé a se you rév . . .
Agau soti lâ Guinê!
Li vôté, li grondé!

(The thunder booms . . . Agau went to Guinea!
The fish come flying,
the sky is the sea
and the sea is a dream . . .
Agau went to Guinea!
He blows, he roars!)

Someone places a knife in Zulé's bare hand and she grasps the rough wooden handle. In the confusion of shouts and good-byes, she sees the emaciated face of Anacaona:

"It will rain fish in the afternoon and that means certain death. Defend yourself while you can."

They never have embraced and won't embrace now. But Zulé knows that if she looks at this woman of sand a moment longer, she will crumble away before her eyes. That is why she turns her back, that is why she pretends once again she doesn't care about her.

"We're leaving, let's go!"

The truck pulls away, dilapidated and noisy, raising a cloud of dust and bagasse fibers. The air still smells of wet salt, and wet salt, at that time of year, invariably smells to them like fresh blood.

T HE CANE FELL SICK that year. A few months before the milling began, the fields were covered by a
white nap that smelled of swamp, and the stalks changed color
and shed their skins like snakes. Two men from the mill came to
see what had happened: they cut segments of cane, took samples
in glass vials, and left again, dizzy with the stink of rotting sugar
cane juice coming from the canebrakes.

They returned a week later and talked at length with the
overseers. The overseers, in turn, emptied the barracks and gathered the workers together in the cleared space in front of the
batey. The harvest was suspended, they could go and see for
themselves what was left of the cane: a field of stalks doubled
over with disease and a plague of rabid mongooses that attacked
anything in their path. Starting now, and until this crop had been
destroyed, they ought to look for work somewhere else. There
was nothing more to say.

From then on an abject, defeated silence hovered over the Colonia Engracia batey. Only a few weeks had passed since the crowning of Zulé, but nobody was thinking about her triumphant return or the gifts she had brought from Mandinga: a pink pig in a wooden crate that they adorned with flowers, and perfumed soap for washing their hair. She left again with Coridón and wasn't there when the men from the mill came to burn the cane. They set the fires at the four most distant points and all the fields burned in a single foul, villainous flame that spewed into the batey a pack of mangy dogs, dozens of singed cats, and the infamous plague of mongooses. When the first howls were heard and the first animals raced past, somebody gave the order to lock up the huts and wooden shacks. The barracks were bolted on the inside by the same men who endured the sight of smoke and the misery of being locked in for two days. Then they opened the doors: the dogs and cats had disappeared, but the mongooses remained, hiding in corners, gnashing their teeth, and attacking day and night for the sheer pleasure of biting.

Zulé hurried back from the Colonia Azote batey, accompanied by Coridón and María Caracoles, and by the Chinese-looking shadow of that adulterated, silent black who didn't leave her side for an instant: Jérémie Candé. They organized sweet toques for the most serene mysteries to see if they might intercede with the ones who had gone mad. They prepared charms and protections, they applied the unbearable green powder remedy to the painless bite marks left by the animals. Then the great flight began, entire families leaving for other bateys, preferring to die of hunger on the road than to go on sleeping in the Colonia Engracia batey under the constant threat of poisonous gnashing teeth.

One afternoon María Caracoles came over to her husband and showed him her leg: the half moon of the wound, three black dots

above, and a whitish break in the skin below. It was hardly notice-
able, but even so they had to bind her, tie her hands behind her,
and urgently begin the cure. She shouted and spat curses at
Coridón while they dusted on her torture. She maintained her
natural affability only with Zulé, who held her head and from
time to time gave her a tiny piece of sugar cane saved from the
disaster, so that she could suck on it. In a few days the fever began, the fever of María Caracoles and of so many others who had
been bitten. And in even fewer hours the rest of the symptoms
appeared: they rolled their eyes, bellowed like cows giving birth,
and attempted, finally, to assault those who were caring for them.
There weren't enough ropes and cords in the batey to tie down
the possessed, and for three days and nights all you could hear
were their unbearable screams as they begged for death. Not a
drop of rain fell and the heat was desperate, and the sick were
taken outside and tied into hammocks under the trees. At night
fires were lit to frighten away the few mongooses still in the
batey. Most had run off to the drying sheds at the mill or been
killed by the rat poison mixed with flour that the Health
Department distributed when it was already too late.

Almost at the end of her agony, María Caracoles tried to bite
Zulé's hand, and this was when Jérémie Candé made a desperate
decision that in a few hours would be imitated by dozens of men
from Colonia Engracia. He went into Papa Luc's shack, found the
machete hanging on the door, and before anybody had time to
guess his intentions, he walked back to his stepmother and
slashed her throat with one clean, merciful stroke. There was
shouting and weeping, and two men ran to take the machete out
of his hands. Only his father, Master Coridón, realized immediately that what his son had done was the most prudent, kind, and
honorable action that could be taken under the circumstances.

"Those are things Chinamen do," he said in a resigned way to Zulé, and he ordered the burial of his wife.

Gradually, with varying degrees of dissimulation, the remaining victims received the compassionate caress of steel. In the batey there was no authority and no desire to stop the slaughter: the infected would die in any case, and it was better to spare them the final spasms, the onslaught of hallucinations, the horror of seeing themselves turned into demons in the final moment of lucidity that would come to them before they died.

After they were all dead and buried, the survivors looked at one another and saw themselves for the first time as what they really were: faded, bony ghosts devoured by lice and stupefied by tragedy. Coridón invited Zulé's family to move with them to Colonia Azote, but Papa Luc and Anacaona and the grown children of the late Jean-Claude did not want to go. They would endure what they had to endure until the drought broke and the cane fields came back to their senses. Papa Luc and the older boys would clear land in La Romana or harvest pineapples outside Bonao, and earn a few pennies to send to Anacaona. In the meantime, she and the youngest child would live on the small amount of cassava they still had in the ground, a few handfuls of blighted flour, and above all, on air.

Coridón took this opportunity to announce his coming marriage to Zulé. But no one was surprised or asked any questions. After all, they had lived for some time as a couple, happy and grateful for the inexplicable tolerance of María Caracoles. In Colonia Engracia there was nothing else to save, no mystery who had not been invoked, no toque that had not been played to the end during the perilous nights of the plague. On the eve of Zulé's departure with her new family, Anacaona woke before dawn, disturbed by sounds that reminded her of the frenetic noise made by the mongooses. Afraid they had returned, she got up stealthily, looked for a light, and left the house without making noise so as not to awaken Papa Luc. Beside the empty corral that was used as a garbage dump she found them, motionless now: on his back, Jérémie Candé; perspiring and erect, sitting on him like a queen on her true throne, was Zulé. Neither one heard her approach, and she herself decided to pierce the night with her bird's voice.

"I can tell."

Zulé jumped up and Jérémie Candé ran off in terror. Anacaona held a small lantern that barely lit the two of them, but the sorry little light was enough to see that the hunger of recent days had not ravaged the splendid body of the woman who would be in command.

"I can tell you're rotten, Zulé. Coridón will kill you."

Zulé did not respond. She merely wiped her forehead with the back of her hand and groped along the ground for the faded dress she usually slept in.

"Doing it with his own son . . . What will you tell him if you get pregnant?"

She spoke in whispers, making it impossible to communicate her anger. Zulé touched her own belly and moved forward until she was almost embracing her stepmother:

"I'm already pregnant."

Having her so close, Anacaona could smell the acrid odor of the man who had just run into the fearful dark of the batey. She wondered if Coridón would smell it too when Zulé returned, honey-sweet and satisfied, from the bottomless pit of her recklessness.

"Suppose it comes out Chinese, like its grandmother?"

"I don't know yet how it'll come out," Zulé replied.

Anacaona turned off the lantern and snorted in the dark:
"I just hope it doesn't look like either one of them."

Papa Luc's first grandchild was born on Ash Wednesday, when
Coridón's Gagá was already organizing its Holy Week celebra-
tions. Anacaona traveled from the Colonia Engracia batey to see
the child and bring him a present of the jute robe that his grandfather had worked with tobacco and turpentine to ward off the
evil eye.

"I got my wish," she told Zulé when she saw the baby. "He
doesn't even look like his mother."

The boy was given the name Florvil Coridón, but he didn't
keep it for very long. A few days after the birth they realized he
hardly ever cried, and showed the whites of his eyes every time
his mother tried to nurse him. Zulé didn't go out with the Gagá
that year. By then her son was near death, and Jérémie Candé
helped her care for him during two nights of torture, until dawn
of Easter Sunday, when the infant stopped breathing.

They buried him in the Yerba Buena cemetery because
Coridón bought a decent coffin and refused to bury him on the
outskirts of the batey, where their other dead were buried, for
fear the dogs would dig him up. To comfort his wife, who did not
shed a single tear or say a single word, Coridón promised to make
her a new baby for the following year. She deigned to look at him
for the first time since the burial.

"No more babies!" she shouted.

And she kept her promise. From then on she found it necessary not only to refuse her husband occasionally but to abandon
Jérémie Candé completely. In silence she tolerated the advances of
her stepson, who could not accept the situation and grew thin
circling round her like a soul in torment; but on the night he

threatened to tell Coridón everything she attacked like a wild animal, gave him a savage slap, and threw in his face the words that left him humiliated and crazed forever.

"Those are things Chinamen do!"

Jérémie Candé never begged again for the crumbs of a love he always saw as far above him—Zulé never changed her mind—and he didn't pursue her at night or go after her when she was alone. The only habit he kept was spying on her and Coridón on the very few nights when the houngan of Azote had his way and threw himself like a lunatic onto the body so often denied him. Zulé knew Jérémie watched them through some crack, and she allowed him to find relief that way, offering him the unbearable view of her gratified face, a shameful spectacle in which Coridón, an old, lazy snake, remained motionless for hours on end, exhausting his prey, swallowing her slowly, digesting her with shrewd, bloodshot eyes.

On only one occasion, many years later, was Zulé careful to close doors and windows, cover the spaces between the planks, and seriously warn Jérémie Candé that she would not let him watch. This was when Similá Bolosse came to Colonia Engracia before trying his luck in the bateys of Boca Chica. Coridón was dead by then, and Zulé cured all the sores on the newcomer with the well-established miracle of her tongue. Then the bokor of Paredón went away and nothing more was heard of him until he had become master of the Gagá in Colonia Tumba, stallion for Olisá Bayí, warhorse for Caé Samá, and voice, body, and pure blood for his most frequent and persistent rider, who could be no other than the one called Bull Belecou.

THEY HAVEN'T STOPPED singing since they left
Colonia Engracia. Honoré Babiole is famous for knowing
many songs, thousands of songs, all the songs made up in the
Dominican Republic as well as ones brought from Haiti. Wild,
fierce songs. Songs no one ever dares to confuse. Which is why he
only has to hum the first few notes and the musicians follow with
the sobbing breath of their bamboos:

> *Ou mande batay . . .*
> *Legbá Manosé anonse m*
> *ou te mande batay . . .*
> *Lanuit la kè popoz*
> *na devore kè w.*

> (You want war . . .
> Legbá Manosé told me

you wanted war . . .
Tonight we'll devour
your heart in peace.)

Zulé Revé, because she is the mistress, rides in front, sitting between the driver, a Dominican from El Cercado, and Jérémie
Candé, who stares avidly out the window. But gusts of Honoré
Babiole's thundering voice reach her inside the truck, and from
time to time she too starts to sing a song that is like the peniten-
tial summation of all the songs she has ever heard.

They go up through Hato Mayor to take advantage of the
good road, but then they veer south and don't stop until they
reach Guayabo Dulce. At the entrance to the town they notice a
strange disturbance, and when they try to climb down from the
truck the elders are overcome by laughter: they have just seen the
War Queen of Elías Piña's Gagá, a mangled crown sliding down
over her eyes as she threatens them, shouting she will kill them if
they take another step, waving the red flag to incite the nation.
Master Elías Piña rushes over and reprimands her harshly, and
then hurries to greet the leaders of Zulé's Gagá. Honoré Babiole,
to frighten him a little, continues singing his battle song:

Ou mande batay . . .
Se sa Legbá Manosé te anonse m.
Ebyen! Nap jete lang ou
bay kayiman manje.

(You want war . . .
Legbá Manosé told me so.
All right! We'll feed your tongue
to the caymans.)

Elías Piña's Gagá has no elders. And everybody knows that a Gagá without elders cannot excel. Even worse are the musicians, so emaciated they can barely carry the weight of their tamboras. The story of this master is known by heart in all the bateys of the country: when he crossed the border, dripping snot from his nose and crying with hunger, people estimated he couldn't be more than two or three years old. Since he came alone and couldn't speak, they gave him the name of the town where they found him. After ten years, Elías Piña left Elías Piña to work as a cane cutter at one of the mills in the south. That was where he joined the Societé of a crippled mambo who allowed him to be initiated without paying a cent in exchange for cooking her food, carrying her in his arms from place to place, and doing all the dirty work in her houmfort. When he was an adult Elías Piña established his own Gagá, if you could call it that—a band of unruly clowns who scattered in every direction before Holy Saturday dawned.

"How do you good people fare?"

He greets everybody the same way, with words he learned as a little boy from the lips of a half-crazed beggar with whom he shared shelter and food for many years.

Honoré Babiole, leaving his songs for the moment, answers the best he can:

"Expecting the bad ones, Elías. We good people are expecting the worst people to show up."

Since the War Queen is still screaming behind him, swearing that no Gagá but her master's will enter Guayabo Dulce, Elías Piña calls a halt and orders her bound. She falls down and writhes on the ground, possessed by a murderous trance and promising to drink the blood of all her enemies. Then, with a great uproar, the women flock around to watch the outcome. Honoré Babiole remains silent: he suspects that this man has things to tell him, and he waits patiently for him to finish imposing order on that chaotic mob.

"At dawn they were on the banks of the Caganche," Elías Piña says at last, savoring the plug of tobacco the musicians have just given him. "Similá Bolosse is carrying pistols, and he swore he'd break the Gagá of Colonia Engracia and kill its mistress with his own hands. He bathed in blood on the other days. By God he did."

"The bath is old news," Honoré Babiole replies.

"What isn't old news"—the other man instantly bristles—"is that his elders all stayed in Colonia Tumba . . . The men with Similá aren't his men but macoutes from Port-au-Prince who crossed a few days ago at Jimaní."

Zulé's Gagá is preparing to begin the pilgrimage and solicit offerings door-to-door. When they finish in Guayabo Dulce they'll take the same highway down to Los Chicharrones, where they'll spend the night.

"If your mistress doesn't change her route, they'll kill her near the Angelina. That's where it will happen."

Papa Luc, on the other side of the road, shakes the whip and asks Honoré to hurry. The musicians, who are about to explode, call for him too, offering him the bottle from a distance and promising him a chew of tobacco if he'll start the songs and guide them to the spirit.

"Anything else?"

Elías Piña scratches his head and looks at his War Queen all covered in dust, her buttocks bared in the agitation of the trance, but moving so little now that he gives the order to untie her.

"There's something else. Similá says he'll cut your throats, you and your brother Truman Babiole, because you're bigmouths."

A Gagá without elders cannot excel. Everybody knows that.

There is a reason why the women spend months sewing and coloring the handkerchiefs, hanging them in clusters from belts, embroidering teardrops of purple glass and reddish-black caravans of beads onto jute neckbands. For when Good Friday dawns and the elders adorn themselves and an unflinching sun falls on the raw fantasy of their bodies, that is when the Gagá sparkles and flowers.

"They beat Truman Babiole with clubs," Elías Piña adds. "Maybe they killed him."

Papa Luc, sadly sensing the end of the world, comes for his comrade, who stands paralyzed and mute before the ragged hosts of the other Gagá.

"We have to go," he says softly, taking him by the arm.

Honoré Babiole allows himself to be led away without thanking Elías Piña or giving another glance at the brash queen, who has in her favor only a display of buttocks as hard and polished as two stones in the river. The musicians, when they see him approaching, ask him to begin with whatever he likes best, and from his chest he draws out the raw voice that once again shakes the red entrails of the earth:

> *Legbá Manosé,*
> *bon m santi m anraje,*
> *Legbá . . .*

> (Legbá Manosé,
> now I'm mad with rage,
> Legbá . . .)

A FEW MONTHS BEFORE he died Coridón had a sudden inspiration, and he woke Zulé in the middle of the night and whispered to her as if he were half asleep. If he passed on one day soon, there were two things she had to do: the first was to found her own Gagá, not in Colonia Azote but down in Colonia Engracia, and fatten it with all the elders, queens, and musicians he would leave adrift; the second was to marry Jérémie Candé.

As soon as he had spoken he went back to sleep, not without first trying to penetrate the protective wall that closed all its gates and no longer allowed itself to be loved. But the next day, when she served him his food, he repeated what he had said, word for word, in the same afflicted voice.

"I'll found my own Gagá," Zulé replied. "But I wouldn't marry your son even if I was crazy."

Coridón looked up from his plate and delivered a blow like a stone to her forehead:

"Then tell me, why do you let him watch?"

She not only let him watch, but there were nights when she made sure to wake Jérémie Candé if he happened to fall asleep before the two of them went to bed. Zulé would leave Coridón on some pretext and hurry to her stepson's cot:

"Now you can . . ."

He would barely open his slanted eyes, leap out of bed, and just as he was, naked and staggering, leave the shack and squat down behind the boards that faced his father's bed. There he would watch them make love, Coridón more and more ardent, Zulé imperturbable and rigid.

"I let him because Anacaona always let me watch her and Papa Luc. Don't you remember, Coridón?"

Coridón remembered, and if she had been alive, María Caracoles would have remembered too. Many years earlier, when they returned to Colonia Azote after taking Zulé from Colonia Engracia, the first thing the girl asked was that they let her see them at night. Coridón knew right away what she wanted, but María Caracoles didn't understand and Zulé had no trouble explaining it to her:

"Anacaona lets me see everything when she goes to bed with my father."

The master's wife finally understood, and contrary to all expectations she burst into laughter and kissed the girl on both cheeks. That night she not only allowed Zulé to watch but invited her to sleep with them. Coridón, seeming smaller than ever, didn't fall asleep for a long time, as if he were bewildered by the terrible satisfaction of having enjoyed both women.

A week later, Zulé repeated that she wanted to watch. Coridón, who knew what she meant this time as well, did his best to dissimulate:

"You see enough of us."

But she insisted. She wasn't talking about their lovemaking. She wanted to see the other thing. The other thing the oldest houngans talked about with reluctance; the other thing you couldn't even guess at with the eyes of this world: she wanted to see the natural landscape of all the dead.

Coridón flew into a rage: she had just come to Colonia Azote, she was a girl with a future, and that's all she was. She hadn't made her baptism, her trial, or her vow. She wouldn't have the strength to go through it. And he didn't intend to return her to Papa Luc a crazy woman, among other reasons because he suspected that Papa Luc would never take her back.

"Your father won't want you and I won't want you either. If you go crazy I'll give you a tin can and throw you into the cane fields."

Zulé had a fleeting vision of what she would become: a filthy creature lying at the side of the road, begging for a slice of cassava and drooling at the sight of a piece of wormy herring. That's what the crazy man Degaulle Aguiné did, a cutter from Cap Haïtien who had been in his right mind until he was devastated by his first Dead Time. And then he hung a can around his neck so that people could throw in food and howled like a dog at the entrance to the barracks.

"But I want to see," she shouted in spite of everything, looking out of the corner of her eye at the strongest and weakest master in the country.

It finally fell to María Caracoles to persuade her husband that he should work the eyes of Papa Luc's daughter. Her argument was simple and brief: if Zulé happened to go crazy, she'd be responsible for taking care of her until the girl returned to her senses.

"She probably never will," Coridón warned, though he knew in his heart that the two women had won the game.

It was during those months that the master began to fear the voraciousness of his pupil. She was no longer satisfied with his authorizing a vision of the double ground of life. She also wanted to know how he accomplished it. Coridón proved inflexible on this point. He put both of them, Zulé and María Caracoles, on the bed and promised to send them down to the dead if he ever caught them spying on him. María Caracoles feared few things in life, but the possibility of going down to the place of the dead and sleeping there forever so terrorized her that she began to scream in dread and swore to her husband she would never bring up the subject again. Papa Luc's daughter remained silent and did not swear anything to anybody. Much later, when Coridón had only a few months to live, she proved to him that from that time on she had known how to do the work, that she had always known how to do the work.

On the same night that new light was given to Zulé's eyes, a sweet, sensual toque was dedicated to the most subtle metresas in the Pantheon. As soon as she heard the intense whisper of the tatúas, Zulé fell into a writhing trance filled with a wild animal's roars and harsh grunts. It was a prolonged trance that frightened everyone except Coridón. María Caracoles, who had promised to take care of her if she went crazy, fell into a panic and begged her husband to stop.

"It's too late," he said, and continued working diligently over the eyelids of the girl who wanted to see more.

When Zulé came to she was content and serene. She remembered nothing of what had happened. She didn't even remember asking Coridón to work her eyes. A little after midnight, she and María Caracoles shared a sweet flour porridge that the master prepared to help them regain the strength lost in the ceremonies. They slept as they always did, the three of them in the same bed, and they woke as they did every day: Coridón curled around Zulé's improbable body and María Caracoles embracing them both. It was at that precise moment, when she opened her eyes and confronted the eternal snare of the batey, that Papa Luc's daughter realized she had taken the most terrifying and terrible step of her life.

She attempted to hide her feelings and helped María Caracoles with breakfast. But the master was on his guard and did not tremble, he did not even look up when Zulé let out a battle cry and threw herself against the walls of the house. Between the two of them, Coridón and his wife managed to carry her to the bed, and there they tied her down and placed wet cloths on her forehead. Papa Luc's daughter, her eyes rolling and astonishment washing over her face, shrieked that she saw snakes, water snakes slithering along the beams in the ceiling.

"What else?"

The floor was covered with deep black snails, the size of a fist, that were slowly climbing the walls of the house. She saw her mother, or what remained of her; she saw her brothers, rotted and wild, playing with bottom mud and serving the loas of the river, two loas who answered to the same name, both of them called Simbí; and she saw her grandmother, her mass of disheveled hair flying in the liquid green of the river that had carried her off to the invincible blackness of Mayombe Hill.

"Tell me what else . . ."

She saw a small yellow woman kneeling on a cushion embroidered in gold thread, pawing at her groin and pulling out live worms.

"Jérémie Candé's mother," Coridón mumbled with no hesitation. "She must have died."

Keeping her promise, María Caracoles tended to Zulé and took care of feeding her. There was nothing that Coridón or anybody else could do to rescue the girl from her nightmare. And so they eventually grew accustomed to her uncontrolled fits of weeping and her impenetrable babbling with the dead. Coridón insisted that for as long as this lasted, Zulé had to sleep alone on a cot they placed next to Jérémie Candé's straw mattress. Every night María would undress her and then tie her down, singing to her softly, promising her presents when the deviltry passed, licking her face until she was asleep. Jérémie Candé, who had barely paid attention to her until then, found himself obliged to cover her mouth when she howled and restrain her whenever she threatened to overturn the cot. One night, when she woke earlier than usual, María Caracoles discovered that her stepson, without even untying the second-sighted girl, was sleeping on top of her. From then on Zulé's visions became less and less frequent, and often two or three days would go by when she didn't see anything except what everybody else saw: the batey boiling in the May heat and steam rising from fields cooking in silence.

Several weeks later she returned to Coridón's bed, where she was welcomed with the usual hospitality. She had emerged from her journey wasted and wise, and she devoted herself so feverishly to doing the work that María Caracoles had to go on caring for her because at times she forgot to eat, and when she fell into too long a trance she forgot the way to the latrines and would spend hours lying in her own filth.

She began at the bottom, preparing protections and paquetes

for the cutters in Colonia Azote, and as time passed people from the surrounding area were asking her to make offerings and arrange burials. One afternoon a woman came from El Seibo and handed her a roll of bills: she wanted an amarre on both of them, on her Dominican husband and that slut from Miches who had stolen him from her. Zulé made a decision that Coridón approved in silence: for the moment she would not take a penny. She asked only for a sweat-stained shirt that belonged to the adulterer, and for two days and nights she worked before the master's altar. When the woman returned for her charm, Zulé gave her a candle the color of dried meat and a black purse to bury under any road the lovers walked on. That was all. The woman came back in ten days, in a rush because she had her husband at home, as docile and penitent as a nursing baby. Then Zulé charged her a fee, and with the money she proposed to Coridón that they hold a toque for the most recalcitrant petrós. After that she wanted to visit her family in Colonia Engracia, and Coridón gave her two chickens to take as a present for Papa Luc. And while she was there, he said, she could invite him to the crowning.

"Who's being crowned?" Zulé feigned ignorance.

"You know who," the master replied. "You know we're crowning you next month in Mandinga."

María Caracoles went with her to her father's house, and as soon as they arrived at the batey, Anacaona cut the birds' throats and cooked lunch. At dusk an exhausted Papa Luc appeared, making a great fuss and happy to see his daughter again. But the fervor in his soul and the confusion in his heart did not prevent him from realizing that the girl had come very far.

"Your eyes were worked with crust from the eyes of dogs," he guessed correctly when Zulé said she had seen her mother, her dead brothers, and even her grandmother trying to swim in the river.

He took her aside and asked for more details, and to please him she described the snakes she had seen on the ceiling and the flood tide of dark snails that had climbed her legs.

"That Coridón," Luc Revé said warily. "What would he have done if you went crazy?"

Zulé burst out laughing and told him everything she knew:

"He would have hung a can around my neck and put me in the cane fields."

On their way back to Colonia Azote, María Caracoles remarked that any day now Coridón would ask her to marry his only son, Jérémie Candé. Zulé shook her head:

"I wouldn't marry the master's son even if I was crazy."

To tell the truth, he didn't ask her to do that until death was hard on his heels. Then Zulé repeated what she had already told the late María Caracoles, and Master Coridón, with that double edge he had on his tongue and in his soul, sought out her eyes and stunned her with his prediction:

"Then watch out for the one who'll come later," he mumbled with his ruined throat. "He has three balls, like the black beast of Jacmel. Watch out for his seed."

O N T H E W A Y O U T of Los Chicharrones there is a
settlement called Manoguayabo, and in the middle of
the settlement is a huge open structure, like a shed for drying tobacco, with a broken sign that sways gently over the panting
countryside: Tight Chests Loosened. It is the house of the healer
Lino the Haitian, who is not Haitian but Dominican, and who
usually provides lodging for Zulé's Gagá when they spend the
night in the hamlet.

This year, the mistress has brought him a gift of a bottle of
rum and a pair of jeans, and he, who was expecting the group, has
lit a fire in the middle of the courtyard and cooked a stew for his
visitors. Lino the Haitian owes two great favors to Papa Luc's
daughter. First and most important, she saved his life when his
healer's arts could not stop the frenzy of blood that rose to his
head, exploded in his eyes, and plummeted to his chest with a

pain like a spike in his living flesh. Zulé was brought to the shed as quickly as possible, and when she arrived the sick man had become rigid and was barely breathing. The people from the settlement said afterward that Lino the Haitian had been a corpse for some time and only the power of a determined and serious mambo like her could have brought him back to life.

The second favor was an amarre. The man who owned the land where Manoguayabo stood had been threatening to evict the residents. Lino the Haitian turned again to Zulé, and she ordered them to bring her a sweaty article of the man's clothing, some nail cuttings, and a lock of his hair for her to work. There was nothing else to do but hire a girl from Los Chicharrones, who asked for fifty pesos and one of Zulé's protections to spend the night with him and steal the things they needed. Now the wretched man came through the settlement every two or three months, repeating without conviction the same useless harangue: they should get ready to be evicted, the police would come soon . . . But it went no further because he had become absent-minded and weak, and suffered from an unpredictable hoarseness that took away his power of speech and then gave it back again. Those had been two great favors, the kinds of favors that had to be paid for with blood. And Lino the Haitian was a grateful man.

"Similá's people had a celebration in Caganche."

He comes out with it quickly, right after they've exchanged greetings and the leaders of the Gagá are settling down around him and Zulé, and he, to welcome them, has offered country clairin, which is simply aguardiente distilled with wild plants on the Island of Gonave.

"They had a celebration in Caganche," he repeats as he stirs the stew. "And then they climbed into their trucks and didn't stop until they got to La Cubana. That's where they'll spend the night."

Papa Luc and Jérémie Candé have not taken their eyes off the dark syrup of the stew. And Honoré Babiole, sitting in a hammock, continues to rub his feet as if he hadn't heard a single word.

"If they're in La Cubana it means they've changed their route."

The mistress tries to maintain a voice of stone, but she can't hide the thread of hope that betrays her. There is still a possibility that Similá Bolosse will decide at the last minute not to have a confrontation with her.

"Don't have any false hopes, Zulé. That black man is on fire."

The voice of Lino the Haitian sounds as deep as the voice of a saint, and his skull-like profile, leaning over the steam rising from the pot, looks as if it will vanish at any moment.

"He's coming with tonton macoutes who sneaked across the border at Pedernales."

"It was at Jimaní," Honoré Babiole interrupts. "Elías Piña said that's where they came in."

"Wherever it was, they're coming to eat people, aren't they? And you, Zulé, you'll be the first one they eat."

Lino the Haitian opens his bottle, and before taking the first swallow he baptizes the thick peace of the stew with a long stream of rum.

"All of you have to stay here. There's no way you can go on."

Honoré Babiole gets to his feet and claims the bottle with a fierce gesture. Then he passes it to Zulé, who drinks like a mad woman, letting half the rum dribble from the sides of her mouth.

"Not even God can stop me now," she shouts, abruptly lifting her inflamed face.

The rest of the men in the Gagá have been drinking since they stopped in Los Chicharrones, and several elders have passed out, not eating a mouthful. But the musicians stay awake, piercing the night with their frenzied drumming. Lino the Haitian has to drink at least half a bottle in order to tell them the rest. Similá Bolosse, he says at last, has blamed Mistress Zulé for the loss of a shipment he planned to take out through Las Cañitas. His old bosses from Paredón, and the bosses of his bosses, who are the big bosses in Port-au-Prince, came to demand an explanation. That was when they all met in the army barracks at Belladere and decided to get rid of the bigmouth Haitian who ruined the deal.

"That's you," says the healer, pointing a skinny finger at Zulé's imposing head.

She squats down to look closely at the intense brilliance of the fire and raises her voice, as if she wanted to make herself heard in the next world:

"From San Pedro de Macorís to Sabana del Mar, from Bayaguana to El Seibo, all the bateys have turned against him. Similá knows he can't rule me, not me."

"He says he had to leave the shipment in the middle of the road," adds Lino the Haitian. "He says it's your fault he lost it."

"Maybe that's what he told his friends the macoutes," Papa Luc suddenly intervenes. "The truth is he got his grass out at Granchorra and sent it on to Puerto Rico."

By now no one should have been surprised at the unexpected knowledge of Zulé's father. But this time even his own daughter is amazed at what she hears.

"Granchorra," exclaims Lino the Haitian. "That's very far away . . ."

There's a reason they say in the batey that Papa Luc hears

everything no matter where the words are said. Mistress Zulé has always known this, and she envies his talent. Envies him in the good sense, because she has inherited her own gifts.

"That's right, Granchorra," Luc Revé says vehemently. "And I'll say it to Similá's face when I meet him on the road: the shipment was saved and Zulé's not to blame for anything."

Jérémie Candé hands the mistress a large bowl brimming with stew, and she begins to eat without appetite, to please Lino the Haitian, who has been staring at her for some time, then staggers to a spot right in front of her and sobs with anger.

"You're stubborn, Mistress Zulé. But that's nothing new. What surprises me is that you're dragging so many people into a fight you can't win."

He has gambled everything, and he stands rigid, nailed to the ground, waiting in vain for the storm. Papa Luc and Jérémie Candé are on the alert, and Honoré Babiole, stirring his aching bones once again, comes to her defense:

"We're all here because we want to be, Lino. The mistress told us before we left that Similá's people had pistols."

"What she didn't tell you," the healer dares to go on, "is that you'll be fighting with flesh and blood macoutes like in Haiti, just like there."

Zulé covers her face with her hands and swallows her tears in silence. When everything is over and they return in peace to Colonia Engracia, she'll remember this night as a horrible nightmare: a fearful storm when the wind ripped off pieces of tree trunks and Baron Samedí, more quarrelsome and belligerent than ever, tore through the countryside to slaughter Christians.

"What a fucking life," Honoré Babiole says with a deep sigh and sits down again because his ankles can no longer support him.

"You're going to die!" Lino the Haitian burst into tears, sentimental, at a loss for words, and drunker and more afflicted than he has ever been in his life.

"If I have to die, I'll die," Zulé replies, opening her hands and showing a false face that doesn't belong to her or anybody else.

After this the entire Gagá comes together and the night passes peacefully. Jérémie Candé, who has barely opened his mouth since they reached Manoguayabo, proposes to another of the elders that they take turns standing guard at the entrance to the settlement. They're very close to the domain of Similá Bolosse, and though they know for a fact that he's spending the night in La Cubana, nobody can be sure he won't turn up suddenly in a sneak attack.

Holy Saturday dawns clear and hot, with a dizzying sun that comes up like a barrage of stones. But they are late leaving the settlement because Lino the Haitian wants to work Zulé's crown. Papa Luc tries to dissuade him: her crown has already been carefully worked. But the other man insists: it may be worked by the spirit, but he is going to work in matter. And then he spends more than an hour concealing pieces of razor blades inside the bows and cloth flowers. From now on no one else must touch it. Only the mistress, with utmost care, when she takes it off and puts it on.

Their good-byes are brief and sorrowful. Lino the Haitian has kissed Zulé's cheeks and shaken the hands of Papa Luc, Jérémie Candé, and the limping Honoré Babiole. Since the early hours the musicians have dedicated themselves to a toque less anguished than the one they played last night, and a few minutes before they leave the man who carries the pouch comes to consult with Zulé. She opens it to make certain the white powders have not spilled and the other protections are safe and in their proper places inside the divine bag. Now they begin the most difficult and profitable part of the pilgrimage; they will sweep across the sugar plantations on this side of San Pedro: the Quisqueya, the Consuelo, the Angelina . . . On the Angelina, according to Elías Piña, Similá will be waiting for Zulé.

"On the way back you'll tell me about it," Lino the Haitian whispers, lost in thought, his eyes still fragile from the ravages of drink.

> *Legbá Manosé,*
> *se pitit ou yo ye . . .*
> *Legbá, ou konnen yo byen.*

> (Legbá Manosé,
> here come your children . . .
> Legbá, you know them well.)

The voice of Honoré Babiole spirals upward like a tornado. And like a tornado it devastates the souls of men.

H E C O M E S F R O M Paredón. He's all bitten by insects."

Zulé Revé, who had just awakened, looked around for Jérémie
Candé and then rested her eyes again on the fleshless, gray profile
of Anacaona. At dawn, before he went out to the fields, it was
Jérémie who woke her, barely whispering her name, bending over
the cot and handing her the pitcher of coffee. She would sit up
without stretching or allowing herself one more moment of
sleep, but then she stayed in bed chewing on a piece of casabe
while he took down his machete, put on his hat, and disappeared
in silence. This is how it had been for more than three years, since
the day Coridón died and she, keeping her promise, moved to
Colonia Engracia to found her own Gagá. She agreed to Jérémie
Candé's accompanying her, but only as an aide and bodyguard.

"He must be a very strong Congo. Not everybody can stand
so much poison in their skin."

That day, for the first time in a long while, it wasn't Coridón's son who woke her at dawn. Anacaona, her father's wife, shook her gently by the shoulders and told her that a bokor, almost naked and with raw, bleeding feet, had come to Colonia Engracia begging them for the love of God to help him.

"He said his name is Similá Bolosse. He has yellow eyes."

When the world turned upside down in Haiti and the big boss fled Port-au-Prince, the bateys in the Dominican Republic filled with macoutes who crossed the border to escape the backlash of revenge. They arrived singed by the fury of the fires and shaken by the howls of their pursuers, and some stayed on and lived in the barracks, especially because the harvest was at its height. But most continued on to the coast and paid to board freighters whose owners agreed to carry them to other islands.

"He says he won't leave without seeing the mistress of the Gagá. Get up so you can send him on his way."

Zulé still couldn't explain why Jérémie Candé had left for the fields without waking her. But the reason was simple: Papa Luc had called him a little after midnight to let him know that the stranger was walking back and forth in front of the mistress's house and had asked to see her before he left. Jérémie Candé and Luc Revé did not sleep that night, nothing was clarified in their conversation with the man, and at daybreak, when they had to go to work, they entrusted Anacaona with keeping an eye on him in case he tried to force his way in.

"Do you know where Paredón is?"

Papa Luc's daughter nodded, her eyes distracted.

"Well, I don't. But your father says it's far away. Haiti's very big, honey."

Zulé remembered immediately. Coridón once mentioned that the bokors who built their temples on the shores of Peligre Lake were supposed to be the most implacable and powerful along the border. Paredón was there, just a step away from the waters of the lake, in the eroded, melancholy shadow of the Black Mountains.

"It doesn't matter where he's from," said Anacaona, "the best thing is for him to keep on going."

The mistress didn't even drink her coffee, among other reasons because nobody brought it to her cot as Jérémie Candé usually did. She tied a skirt around her waist and smoothed down her kinky hair with hands smeared in brilliantine.

"You look like a Haitian with your tits bare," Anacaona grumbled.

When she finally left the house, she saw nothing but the half-deserted landscape she saw every day. In the distance, in the empty field where the women washed clothes, a group of children were playing with what looked like an ash-colored snake. She strained her eyes to see exactly how big the animal was, and at that moment she felt a presence behind her. She knew it wasn't Anacaona because the breathing was different, and she knew it was the stranger because the wind smelled suddenly of muddy boar and a thick-furred animal in its lair.

"Mama Zulé . . ."

He had a mellow voice with its own echo, like a reciter of prayers, and it reminded her of the voice of mysteries she had never heard.

"Mama Zulé, they told me about you in Paredón."

She turned to look at him and saw the yellow eyes her stepmother had mentioned. Similá Bolosse had lowered his shoulders to show humility, and was scratching furiously at the sores on his arms.

"Who told you?"

"The people who go back and forth buying the dead. They

told me about the untamed daughter of a luckless houngan who lived on the slopes of Mayombe; they told me about the dead Coridón's widow, as tough as a man; they told me about the long courtship of a black Chinaman who isn't mute but never opens his mouth. All three times it was you."

She invited him into her house, and when he collapsed onto a stool she put water on to boil for coffee. Similá, watching her out of the corner of his eye, asked for some hot rum to lower his fever, and Zulé came over to him, touched his forehead, and found that it was true: he was burning up. She put a bottle into a double boiler to heat it, and served him the liquor in a bowl with a spoon so he could eat it like soup. The stranger soon tired of such delicacy and began to gulp it down, taking more with each swallow than could fit in his mouth. Anacaona, who watched everything in silence, came close to Zulé and whispered in her ear:

"Get rid of him, I'm telling you. He's a Haitian animal."

Then he began to tell everything as if he were half-asleep. Since the fall of the big boss in Port-au-Prince, this was the first time anybody had treated him like a person. In Paredón they hacked the boss of the macoutes to pieces, and they did the same to the bosses in Rosec, Loma Copra, Baptiste. Then they said they'd kill the bokor Similá Bolosse, and he didn't wait for them to come and find him. He left his house, his altars, and his watchdogs, and ran away to hide in the countryside.

"And your wife?" asked Papa Luc's daughter. "Where did you leave her?"

"I haven't had a wife for a long time," Similá replied. "I had a Dominican wife who went to Monte Cristi before the trouble started. My son Tarzán is there too, but I haven't been able to see them."

As he spoke about his misfortunes he began to fall asleep. He continued moving his lips but the words could no longer be heard, and Zulé shook him before he passed out completely.

"Lie down there."

She directed him to her own bed, under the reproachful eye of Anacaona, who clenched her hands as if she were burning with the desire to slap her. Similá Bolosse staggered to the cot and slept until noon, when he was awakened by the smell of the food Zulé was heating to take to Jérémie Candé. Anacaona had finally left after lamenting the fact that this raw-skinned and broken black had gotten as far as he had.

"He'll infect you," she predicted as she limped away; her legs had grown stiff earlier than those of other women in the batey.

As soon as he opened his eyes, Similá Bolosse asked for majá fat to cure his sores, and Zulé offered to spread it on. She finished undressing him herself, pulling off the soiled loincloth that had once been trousers, and then began to rub his burning skin while he moaned because the stings were inflamed. When she had finished with the majá fat, she brought a potion of roots to soften the scabs on his chest.

"Here too," Similá ordered, moving her hand down to his lower belly.

She obeyed, happy to take orders after so many years of only giving them.

"And here!"

Zulé never knew if the man from Paredón said those words or if she sensed them, looking into his eyes, sinking into the sunlit circles of that forbidden glance. The next thing she heard was the thud of her own body as it fell to the dirt floor, helpless and kicking like a turtle on its back. Similá Bolosse slaughtered her just as turtles on the coast are slaughtered, he conquered her among the overturned stools, he subdued her a thousand times, making her kiss the ground. When Zulé, her bones like kindling, was finally able to stand it was late, and most of the women had already left for the fields to take food to their husbands. She set aside some pieces of yam for Similá, wrapped up the rest of the cold food, and headed down the path toward the cane fields. Jérémie Candé was waiting for her next to Papa Luc, who was already eating his lunch in the presence of Anacaona.

"It's hot," Zulé complained, handing over the food under the icy stares of her relatives.

"Your hands stink," said Jérémie Candé. "Of majá fat."

She smelled them as if she doubted his words:

"Fat, that's right. I had to put it on the bokor from Paredón."

They finished eating in silence, and when the overseer began to clap his hands and blow his whistle, Anacaona and her step-daughter walked back together along the path.

"You smeared the fat on him," Anacaona said. "And that viper, Mistress, tell me what the hell he was smearing on you."

Zulé's breasts were still bare, the first time in her life she had carried lunch to the fields without putting on a housedress.

"Everybody's looking at you," Anacaona scolded. "You look like a Haitian. Did you see how hot the overseer was getting?"

Zulé lowered her head and looked at her breasts, as if only then realizing her mistake, and continued walking, feeling con-strained, sure that Anacaona was right: the overseer had been licking his lips, right in her face.

"And besides, my girl, I can tell . . ."

Zulé stopped abruptly to shoo away the green flies from the cane field that always followed her for a time, driven mad by the wake of dirty plates. Anacaona took the opportunity to poke her finger next to the mistress's purplish nipple:

"I can tell he sucked them."

At dusk, when Jérémie Candé came back from the fields, he found Similá Bolosse near the Bower, which at that time of year was almost ready, humming a song from Haiti and draining the water from coconuts. All that Zulé would say was that he had to give up his hammock that night: the man from Paredón was going to stay for three or four days, letting his wounds heal before continuing on to the Colonia Tumba batey.

"If they see him like this, they won't give him work," the mistress reasoned.

Jérémie Candé took down his machete again, put his hat back on his head, and went straight to Papa Luc's wooden shack to humbly ask for lodging.

"Similá has a long tail," Anacaona cried angrily from the stove where she was heating some ears of corn, "and that Zulé has been needing a whip for a long time."

Papa Luc lowered his eyes and then shared his corn with the inscrutable Jérémie Candé. Anacaona, faint with hunger, watched the two of them with a certain envy and then began to suck on her own ear of corn, which was the thinnest of all.

"Too bad you're so Chinese," she concluded, looking sadly at Jérémie Candé.

The next day, when he left the fields, Jérémie went to see Mistress Zulé instead of going directly to Luc Revé's house. The man from Paredón was in the same place, softly singing the same provocative song: *Erzulie, ou mandé kocho / M'apé ba ou li* (Erzulie, you want a hog / I'll give one to you), and drinking the water from all the coconuts he had already deflowered.

"It's good for the middle," he exclaimed, touching the place where his kidneys were, holding a coconut in the air and pouring the whitish stream directly into his throat.

Zulé was inside, picking over a bag of dried peas, and when she heard Jérémie Candé come in she didn't even look up.

"Similá hasn't left yet."

He sat down anyway and helped her clean the peas.

"I know. I came to ask you to let me watch tonight."

She jumped up and a shower of clean peas scattered across the floor.

"You want to watch," she roared, enraged, "and I'm telling you to go back to Papa Luc's and not come near my house. If I catch you watching I'll scratch out your eyes."

He stood up too, extended his hand, and placed it on Zulé's naked breast. Then he twisted the nipple and narrowed his furious slanted eyes. She groaned and slapped his face, and he jumped back, crazed and weeping.

"You let me watch before," he reproached her from the door.

"I'm going to cover the cracks," the mistress warned. "If I find you out there watching, I'll kill you."

Jérémie Candé did not go back to Zulé's house for a long time, among other reasons because Similá Bolosse spent ten days and nights in Colonia Engracia. The mistress hardly went out, and Anacaona had to take lunch to the men in the family. They both became accustomed to listening to the same harangue every day, delivered in varying tones of rancor. That Haitian, Anacaona grumbled, would bring nothing but calamity to the batey. As ragged and covered with sores as he was, just look how the mistress went out of her way to console him.

"I think he put an amarre on her," she muttered between her teeth. "He must have fed it to her on the end of his own tail."

At about this time, a flock of fugitive parrots congregated near the batey. They had nested nearby in the past, but this was the first time they had taken refuge in the ceiba tree on the path to the cane fields, the only ceiba still standing for many kilometers around. There were more than a hundred parrots, and they made the usual racket, but this time they also pulled apart the pods on the tree, filling the air with a white fluff that the cutters would have compared to snow if any of them had ever seen it.

On the eve of Similá's departure, the first, almost insignificant tufts began to fall, and by noon the next day the downpour had become so heavy that the women had to cover their faces like outlaws in order to carry lunch to the laborers. Hidden inside her house, looking out through a crack, Zulé saw Anacaona pass by, covered from head to foot, dragging her lameness as if it were a dead man and muttering curses at the swirling fluff that clouded her sight.

Similá Bolosse, still panting from their farewell lovemaking, wanted to go out to enjoy the landscape of cottony chaos that half the world was navigating through. When he returned, he heard Zulé laugh out loud, the first and last time in ten days he had heard that sound. She brought him a piece of mirror so he could see himself: the flying tufts had stuck to his face, and now he looked exactly like the most feared and rancorous mystery in the Pantheon: it was the face of Bull Belecou. He contemplated his image, solemn and ecstatic, proud because the invincible mask had been returned to him. Then he half-closed his eyes, began to sway back and forth, and sang a song as powerful and light as the storm falling on the countryside:

M'toro m'béglé,
nâ savân mwê . . .
Toro mwê toro, sa ki mâdé pu mwê,
ou a di o
mwê mèm kriminel.

(I am a bull,
I bellow in my savanna . . .
A bull, I am a bull,
and whoever asks for me
tell him I'm a criminal.)

Zulé had given him a pair of jeans and some Dominican sandals, and he had woven a bag of palm leaf to carry over his shoulder. He began to walk away, not saying a word and not wiping the snow from his face, and the mistress followed him to the edge of the batey. They both stopped there and she threw herself to the ground to lick his feet, to humbly embrace his knees, to press her hungry mouth against the secretive snake where the three famous streams of sperm spurted from their triple source and merged into one . . . Then she watched him leave, and now she was covered with the fleece of the winds but did not have enough voice to say his name, enough tongue to call him back, and she was weeping and whorish like Metresa Freda, submissive and great like the Virgin of Erzulie.

I t's Galeona Troncoso's people," Honoré Babiole stammers. "They saw Similá."

It has taken them a very short time to reach the Colonia La
Cacata batey, and as soon as they climb down from the truck a
woman comes to warn them that another Gagá is already making
its way through the settlement. Jérémie Candé and Papa Luc go
to find out exactly who they are, and on the way to the mill somebody tells them that early in the morning he saw Tarzán Similá,
Similá Bolosse's only son, buying food at the grocery. They turn
around and go back to inform the mistress. They talk briefly next
to the truck, and she decides that Jérémie Candé should leave
right away and find out where they are. Honoré Babiole opposes
the idea. Nobody knows Jérémie in La Cacata, and that crafty
Chinese face of his will raise a good deal of suspicion. He, on the
other hand, has friends here who will protect him if necessary.
He's the one who should go.

"You're lame," says the mistress. "They'll beat you with clubs."
Honoré smiles reluctantly.

"What they'll probably do is cure my lameness."

He finally leaves, armed with a machete, and Zulé orders the musicians, the queens, and the rest of the elders, including her own father, to climb back in the truck and wait without making any noise. Only she remains below, accompanied by Jérémie Candé and the Gagá's two guards, who chew a purple tobacco and periodically spit out the dark juice. Half an hour later, when they're thinking about sending another emissary, they see the decrepit figure of Honoré Babiole appear in the distance, shouting words that are lost in his frantic gasping for breath. He stops in front of Zulé and can scarcely find the voice to tell her that the Gagá back there isn't Similá Bolosse's but Galeona Troncoso's, a vengeful, hard-hearted old mambo who has never wanted dealings even with her own shadow. Galeona's people have seen Similá's gang, but that was a while ago, before dawn. Since then they haven't even heard any fututos.

"I tried to talk with that she-devil," Honoré Babiole concludes. "But she told me to say she'll talk only to you, mistress to mistress."

Zulé has a sudden inspiration and asks her people to climb down from the truck and get ready. They'll enter La Cacata with the same jubilation as in other years, and she'll have her talk with the formidable mambo. Jérémie Candé and Papa Luc go off to review battle plans with the musicians and the elders. Honoré Babiole has warned them there may be trouble inside the settlement and from now on they'll have to keep their eyes open. When they finally begin to move, Papa Luc makes a last effort to save his daughter:

"If that scorpion shows up, leave him to the men."

Zulé Revé, who is dancing at the head of the group, doesn't stop to answer him:

"Sure, I'll leave you his bones."

To get to Galeona Troncoso one needs a good deal of patience and great humility, two qualities that have never adorned Zulé's rebellious head. After passing through the town, they stop in front of a shack without an owner or anybody who wants to be the owner, where the altars of Papa Trinidad, a houngan who died of a harmful spell six months earlier, are still smoking. Galeona has taken shelter there, and that is where Zulé goes, asking to see her. The musicians in both Gagás have stopped playing, and the silence is so hateful that Honoré Babiole sings nonsense songs, wheezing with his parched voice.

"Galeona says you can come in."

The guard is missing almost all his teeth and has already drunk enough to stagger without falling down. Zulé straightens her crown, the razor snare that Lino the Haitian prepared for her, and plunges into the fog of a temple that still smells of poisoned blood. Galeona is lying motionless inside a circle of black candles, as if put to sleep by the smoke of her own cigarette. When she hears Zulé approach, she half-opens her eyes and tries in vain to raise her head.

"You already smell like a corpse."

Zulé squats down to look at her. It is just a year since she's seen her, and nothing has changed very much in that face of a human tortoise. What does keep changing is her voice, which grows huskier and more scornful and more strained, as if the collar of her goiter were about to strangle her.

"Since Similá is going to send you straight to the next world, do me a favor, Mistress Zulé, and take a message to Papa Trinidad."

Galeona Troncoso's romance with the man in whose temple she takes shelter now was a long, tempestuous one. They had eight children, all of them stillborn, and when Trinidad left her for another woman, she put an amarre on them both. She drove her rival in love, a good-natured girl from Santiago, out of her mind in ten days; with Trinidad, because he was the guiltier one, she was harsher: Galeona tortured him for years using the malleable hide of a rag doll, and finally stabbed him in the heart, slowly and deeply, with a pin soaked in herring brine so that he would die begging for water. The residents of La Cacata swore that in the small hours they heard moaning inside the shack, and whoever wanted to could see the helpless ghost of the houngan, wandering among his relics and uselessly lighting yellow candles so that his soul could leave his body.

"Tell him for me not to bother Christians anymore, and in case he doesn't know he's dead, it's time for him to stop."

Galeona Troncoso never really lived in La Cacata. In her youth she would stay for a while, make love to Papa Trinidad for a few nights, and then return to her native batey to give birth to her children. She would come back with her Gagá during Holy Week, carrying in her pouch the bare bones of the most recent child she had lost. Then the houngan would become enraged and blame her for the death of the babies.

"Take him that message . . . You can give it to him today, Similá's already on his way."

"Similá isn't going to kill anybody," Zulé replies.

"He'll kill you, girl. You got in the way of the macoutes, and that's not good. You got in the way of their business, and they never forgive anything."

"Similá doesn't rule in my Gagá," says Zulé. "He and the macoutes don't rule anywhere anymore."

Galeona Troncoso has completely lost movement in her neck, and in order to look straight at Zulé she has to turn her entire body, which is as big and slow as a bad dream.

"Where are your brains, little mistress . . . The macoutes still rule in Haiti, and now they're going to rule in the bateys. They have their hideouts here."

The previous year, when Papa Trinidad was still alive, Zulé had visited him in this same temple where she now wishes she could hear the gasping wheeze of his voice. The old houngan was dying and knew that Galeona Troncoso was the cause of all his suffering. But by then he didn't have the heart or the time to feel rancor toward his old lover. He was too worried about the schemes of the Haitians who kept pouring into the batey, hid for a few days, and then disappeared into the countryside. He had seen them waiting for the small planes; he had seen them loading and unloading bundles; he knew all too well about the trafficking that would eventually put an end to peace in the settlements, an end to the secret harmony of the Societés.

"I need your men, Galeona. Let me have them until tomorrow."

"Similá has a pack of macoutes waiting for you in the Angelina."

"You've finished your pilgrimage, let them come with me."

"They're going to kill you, Mistress Zulé. Take this message to Trinidad: tell him that when I tried to unbind him it was too late, the harm was already in his bones."

"Let me have your men and I'll repay the favor."

Galeona struggles to stand but refuses the hand that Zulé offers her. When she is finally on her feet, Papa Luc's daughter doesn't hide her astonishment: the woman can barely breathe, and in the battle to the death to keep her balance, her eyes almost pop out of their sockets and the purplish tip of her tongue protrudes at the corner of her mouth.

"I won't tell my elders what to do. But if they want to go with you, they can."

Zulé leaves the hut immediately, hard and solemn, as circumstances demand, and she doesn't even need to announce Galeona's decision.

"Ten of those men are coming with us," Papa Luc says, pointing at the group. "One of them has a pistol."

She pretends she hasn't heard anything about the weapon and tells them to give two bottles of rum to the other mistress.

"We only have one left," Jérémie Candé discovers.

"Well, give it to her. And a piece of casabe too."

Honoré Babiole takes her aside to talk. He's the one who persuaded Galeona's men to join Zulé's Gagá even before the she-devil gave her consent.

"I'll answer for the elders," he says. "But not for that bitch. If she could put an amarre on Trinidad, the father of her children, what won't she do against you?"

Zulé shakes her head. She is sure Galeona Troncoso will do nothing but stay where she is, trapped forever in the darkness of the shack where even the air refuses to forgive her.

"I don't trust her," he insists. "She's as bad as Similá."

A melancholy, ghost-ridden silence descends. This isn't the moment to remind Honoré Babiole that he is still bleeding from the wound; that many years ago, when Galeona and Trinidad began to make love, he wandered the bateys begging for just one caress from that impetuous mambo, ready to eat the mud she walked on, happy to let himself be humiliated by her savage remarks. The oldest people still remembered the day when Galeona gave birth for the fourth or fifth time. Honoré forced his way into the shack, approached the cot where the mambo was crying over her motionless infant, and shouted that this was happening because she had children by someone who didn't have the balls to father anything but dead babies. Galeona Troncoso never forgave him for that outburst and never allowed him near her again.

"It's time for us to go," says Zulé.

The musicians from both groups have come together as if by instinct, producing a sound so sublime it seems as if they had played in the same Gagá all their lives. The elders have been blowing their whistles for some time, and all the people of La Cacata have come out to watch them depart. At that moment Jérémie Candé passes by, carrying the bottle of rum and a piece of casabe wrapped in brown paper. Honoré, his eyes filled with tears, has a single moment of weakness.

"Bring it here," he says. "I'll take it to her."

An alarmed Jérémie stops, motionless, his hands empty, certain that an ancient misfortune is about to occur. Zulé stands beside him, contemplating the muffled cadence of the steps with which Honoré is sinking into a suddenly reawakened grief.

"Honoré's going to stay here," she murmurs, her heart breaking, her eyes fixed on Galeona's shack. "We have to let him stay."

Papa Luc, who observes them from a distance, comes over ready to intervene, but a sharp glance from Zulé is enough for him to understand that everything is finished, concluded, pulled down by the eternal weight of a decree written in stone.

"We'll be out when it's dark," he warns his daughter.

She looks at the sky, as if conjecturing that night will never fall on them again. The skin on her arms crawls, and she shakes her hands violently to get rid of the miasma of an evil omen that passed too close to her.

"Let's go . . ."

Before climbing into the truck with all the others, she takes a final look at the shack that once belonged to Trinidad and where Mistress Galeona Troncoso is still secluded, dying among the black candles of her grief, at once desired and despised by the only man in this world who could have given her a child that lived. That is, by Honoré Babiole.

DAYS LATER, someone remarked on the coincidence: as soon as Similá Bolosse left Colonia Engracia, the rain of white tufts stopped falling and the parrots nesting in the ceiba lapsed into a deep, inexplicable silence. Zulé locked herself in her shack for three days and in that time did not allow anyone to see her, not even her father, who came night after night to leave her a plate of corn porridge and a pitcher of water with brown sugar that Anacaona prepared for her. Jérémie Candé was prudent enough not even to attempt a return. He resigned himself to hearing the news that Papa Luc brought and scrutinizing the agitated face of Anacaona, who finally blurted it out on the third day:

"All we need is for her to be pregnant."

Jérémie, who hadn't thought of that possibility, could only look at Zulé's father, searching for a denial that would move his feet away from the fire and place his scorched soles back on the ground. But the houngan looked aside and threw more wood onto the flames of his misfortune:

"It's still too early."

A few weeks later, Zulé came looking for her assistant. People had arrived from Santo Domingo to request a delicate piece of work—finding a woman who had gone down to the place of the dead—and for that she needed help. Jérémie listened in silence, his expression as imperturbable as it was when he heard her ordering him to leave. Then he got to his feet, took down his machete, put his work clothes in a bag, and flew like an arrow into the fiery afternoon. Zulé went after him, and Anacaona stood watching until they disappeared in the sultry haze that smelled of boiled tobacco.

"Your daughter doesn't look good," she said to Papa Luc, "and it's hard for her to talk. You can gouge out my eyes if she isn't pregnant."

That night, when Papa Luc and Anacaona were already in bed, they heard Jérémie Candé outside shouting that Zulé was bleeding to death. Papa Luc lit the lantern and stood there paralyzed, incapable of understanding the handful of words that seemed to pass from one ear to the other, leaving a black trail as if they were bullets. When he could finally move again, he begged Anacaona to go out and see what was happening.

"What's happening is what had to happen," she replied calmly. "She's getting rid of the baby."

A horrified Jérémie Candé collapsed onto a stool and gave silent thanks for the glass of rum Papa Luc placed in his hands.

"You see? I was right," grumbled Anacaona. "I told you Similá had a very long tail."

She tended the mistress that night and the two nights that

followed, and when she came back to Papa Luc she made only one bitter, categorical comment:

"That black man's seed is finished."

The topic was not mentioned again for several months. The Dead Time came, and the memory of Similá Bolosse seemed to vanish like the snow from the ceiba. Jérémie Candé left with Papa Luc to work in the sisal fields, and they both made it a habit to return to Colonia Engracia every second Sunday to heal the gashes on their arms and the whitish ulcers that seethed on their faces.

"Cowtongue bites, cowtongue kills," Anacaona muttered when she saw her husband, his cheeks eaten by sores and his clothes in tatters.

"It's work for Haitians," she added, looking at the wounds on his legs that were best cured with applications of spider webs.

Mistress Zulé, absorbed in locating the woman who was making her somnolent way through God only knows what evil places, had little time to spend on Jérémie Candé's injuries. Coridón's son would arrive in silence and in silence smear on the potion of roots and make the jute gloves for closing up his puncture wounds.

"It's work for blacks," Anacaona insisted, looking at the wreckage of those two men who would get up before dawn on Monday, their souls in torment, to go back to hell.

One Sunday, while Zulé was mending clothes and Jérémie Candé dozed on his cot, the sharp, clotted name of Similá Bolosse rose up between them again. Suddenly she mentioned that she would have to take a trip: she had confidential information that the woman she was looking for was in Haiti, specifically in Paredón. She had been seen in a settlement on the shores of Peligre Lake. Jérémie instantly sensed the proximity of the devil, and he opened his narrow eyes.

"I'll have to ask Similá about it," the mistress concluded. "Similá comes from Paredón."

Jérémie took a deep breath and looked at Zulé's hands, which were incapable of trembling even when she went on to say:

"I'll ask him to come with me."

Only a moment before he would have sworn that nothing in this world was more painful than working between rows of mature sisal, surrounded by thorny tongues of agave that pierced the laborers' skin and opened wounds where mosquitoes settled for days at a time. But now he knew he could endure the attacks of cowtongue more easily than Zulé's terrible words.

"I can't go alone," she added. "And you'll be in the fields."

Anacaona was right: cowtongue bit, cowtongue killed without meaning to. And more than any other tongue in this world, Zulé's was the harshest in Haiti, the cruelest and most poisonous in the Dominican Republic. Jérémie leaped to his feet in a rage and planted himself in front of her.

"You're in my light," Zulé complained.

"Why didn't you let me look that night?"

She raised her eyes and saw the distorted face of Coridón's son.

"If you want, I'll let you look now."

Jérémie Candé returned to the cot and watched the mistress pull off her housedress and toss it on the tamped down earth of the floor.

"Is this what you wanted to see?"

She came toward him naked, lifting her breasts with both hands.

"I wanted to see you with Similá."

Zulé stood as if nailed to the floor, watching Jérémie grow big,

moan, howl, and finally water the burning coals of a solitary outburst of passion.

"You can rot there," she spat in his face. "Those are things
Chinamen do."

Similá Bolosse, who by this time was organizing his own Gagá,
did not reply to any of the messages Zulé sent to him at the
Colonia Tumba batey. Truman Babiole, Honoré's brother, person-
ally gave him three: the first, that Mistress Zulé wanted to see
him; the second, that Mistress Zulé wanted to know the easiest
route to Paredón; the third and most direct, that Mistress Zulé
wanted him to go with her to Haiti. Similá responded to all of
them with an icy silence and a fierce look that frightened away
the possibility of more words. That, at least, is what Honoré
Babiole told the mistress when she tried to send a fourth message:
that Similá should tell her the name of some trusted houngan or
mambo who could help her in Paredón.

"My brother Truman doesn't want to take him any more messages. He says Similá is all fired up thinking about important
things; alliances are all he talks about; he's like a big boss now."

Zulé acknowledged defeat and accepted the offer of Jérémie
Candé, who proposed leaving the sisal fields for a few days and accompanying her on the trip.

"If I bring back that woman," she said, "you and Papa Luc
won't have to work again until the Dead Time is over."

Since Similá did not recommend any houngan to guide her,
Zulé appealed to a Dominican well known for his contacts across
the border. Papa Trinidad lived in the Colonia La Cacata batey
and had been Coridón's friend for many years. He had been sick a
long time, due to the effects of a death amarre put on him by a
woman, and he himself would recount his misadventures with

that dangerous, hard-hearted mambo whom he had made pregnant no fewer than eight times. Zulé went to see him and found him in bed, suffering from a raging thirst that no liquid could satisfy and moaning from a pain in his chest that barely allowed him to speak. Yet he found the breath to say there was a houngan in Loma Copra who could be useful to her if she was willing to pay. The man was named Malesherbes Mombin, but everybody called him Horns. There were no secrets for him, not in the region of Artibonite or anywhere else; no devil crossed the border without his knowing it; nobody went down to the place of the dead without immediately coming to tell him about it; there was no bonepot or burial or harmful spell that the famous Horns could not find. If the woman they were looking for was anywhere around there, Malesherbes Mombin had to know about it.

Zulé thanked him for the information and asked Papa Trinidad if she could help him in any way. The houngan shook his head ponderously and looked at her, intoxicated with despair:

"Do you know what's used to undo the amarres of a crafty mambo?"

"It depends on the amarre," she replied.

"The one that Galeona Troncoso put on me can no longer be undone. She cut my nails and took away the parings; she stole my clothes and squeezed out the sweat; she even took the seed for making children from the bed. With all of that, and the blood of her dead babies, which was blood of my blood, she went to see her compadre, a black devil from Jacmel."

Zulé lowered her head but out of pity said there was a remedy for everything.

"Not even you believe that," Trinidad sobbed. "Though I don't care anymore; we have to die of something."

A week later she left with her assistant for Santo Domingo,

where they'd take a bus that would carry them to San Juan, from San Juan to Comendador, and from Comendador to Belladere. After that, going down to Loma Copra would be easy, and once they were in that town, they would deal with the task of finding Horns. Jérémie Candé, mute and happy to be making the trip, didn't even feel uneasy when the mistress mentioned the cursed man.

"One day Similá will want to swallow us up . . ."

They had to stand on the bus, crushed by people and plagued by thirst, but he was feeling so fortunate he dared to place his hand on the unapproachable buttock of the woman who could do anything.

"Some day he's going to want an alliance, and that's the day we'll have a war."

"You'll win," he moaned, just touching her with his fingers.

"I won't win, the dogs will. I'll give Similá's balls to the dogs to eat."

Jérémie knew this would be his only opportunity. He leaned over Zulé's shoulder, moved the hair away from her face, and spoke in a wretched whisper.

"Anacaona says Similá has three. But I don't believe it."

At first she bit her lip and refused to resolve his doubts. But then she changed her mind and placed her hand in front of his Chinese eyes, moving it up and down as if judging the weight of a beautiful fruit.

"I held them here . . . And I swear to you he has three."

O N H O L Y S A T U R D A Y the light has almost faded
when they reach Jimaguas, a settlement located at the
entrance to the Angelina plantation. The new cane cutters,
dozens of untamed Congos still licking their wounds, live there,
along with the men who clean the mill, most of them Haitians
who have not worked in the Dominican Republic for very long. As
soon as milling begins they put in twelve-hour shifts, and when
they leave the mill they bring with them the impassive fatigue of
oxen and the unbearable stink of rotting cane juice. Zulé smells
the odors with a grieving heart. She thinks of Honoré Babiole,
who has stayed behind to watch Galeona Troncoso die, and she
thinks especially of Papa Luc, befuddled by his years and the daz-
zling light of rum. Only Jérémie Candé remains strong, his eyes
shining like two moons onto the sorrowful face of the only
woman in his life.

"Wait for me here," she orders. "And make sure the people don't scatter."

There are hardly any trees around Jimaguas, only some twisted, sickly bushes, a few palm trees sagging in the drought, and the sharp-edged debris from the cane fields blown about by the wind. The rest of the men and women in the Gagá wander the empty field looking for a place to rest their bones. Zulé moves off by herself to contemplate the purplish silhouette of the mill: on the other side of those blackened walls, crouching behind the houses in the batey, Similá Bolosse is waiting for her. And with Similá are the macoutes, ready to fight as soon as the master gives them the battle signal. If she wanted to, she could still change her route, head toward La Luisa and go up along the banks of the Chavón. But her fears are not what count in this ill-fated, foul-smelling hour; what counts are the desires of the Baron of the Cemetery, which are as exacting and unfathomable as the approaching night.

> *Au nom Baron de Cimetiére*
> *guardien de tous les morts,*
> *vous, vous, vous seul*
> *qui traverzes le purgatoire . . .*

> (In the name of the Baron of the Cemetery,
> guardian of all the dead,
> you, you, you alone
> who are crossing purgatory . . .)

Zulé squats down in the weeds and feels nausea trapped in her stomach. Changing the route now would be like breaking the

Gagá she swore to protect from harm and from the brutal hand of men. If she did, then Similá would become the implacable master of the boundary lines, the hidden scourge of almost all the bateys.

> *Negre guedevi, negre ceclay,*
> *negre rousé, negre trois aoux,*
> *trois pince, trois picais,*
> *trois gamelles . . .*

> (Long-haired black living in the devil,
> black digger of graves,
> three-spades, three-picks,
> three-hoes, three-scales . . .)

The perspiration on her face, as thick and hot as blood, rolls slowly down her neck, and she falls backward with the hopeless certainty that she is leaving the world.

> *Negre lenvére,*
> *negre cordon noir,*
> *negre roidou . . .*
> *Ago-Agocy-Agolá . . .*

> (Unruly black,
> black cord black
> black king black . . .
> Ago-Agocy-Agolá . . .)

She writhes, she twists, she flails on the ground. Her eyes bulge with the effort not to see the devil who is coming toward her. It is the *cochon sans poil* himself, his red shadow descending to sniff at her face, her hands, her swollen mouth that does not stop asking why the Baron sends her suffering that is larger, much larger than the hidden stream of her scant tears.

Finally she sits up and gradually discovers that she has been in a profound trance for too long. Night is falling, categorical and desolate, and she decides to rejoin her Gagá, dragging her feet, trying to see in the anguished eyes of her elders which of all the mysteries, of those most ferocious and ignored, has just mounted her.

"Come have a drink," shouts one of the musicians as he raises a bottle full of air.

Zulé does not answer right away. She looks at him and then, one by one, at the torpid faces of her followers.

"Similá is out there," she says biting off her words, "and my elders are asleep . . ."

Several of them are nodding, it is true, chewing on muffled howls from the rancorous depths of their nightmares.

"How could you fall asleep?"

Without the conciliatory powers of Honoré Babiole, it is Jérémie Candé who intervenes to soothe their spirits. The people have no more to give, he tells the mistress, they've been drinking all afternoon and need a rest. The guards of the Gagá are standing watch nearby, but it seems there won't be anything to worry about until midnight. According to what they were told by two laborers who just came from the Angelina, Similá's gang is very drunk.

"That's exactly why," the mistress thunders. "We're going in now."

Papa Luc, who has been lying on a brightly colored blanket, opens his eyes and searches his bleary imagination for the embers that will keep him from shivering. Jérémie Candé, gruff and fearless, dares to argue with her.

"Now, Mistress? It's very late now."

"Let them eat first," she concedes. "But then we're going in."

In the settlement they have been offered a pail of plantains in syrup, and the women of the Gagá begin to heat a chicken stew they cooked before leaving Colonia Engracia and carried in two large blackened cans, the ones they use for boiling clothes. When it is time to eat, Papa Luc convenes the elders and speaks to them in a solemn voice: the mistress has decided to go into the Angelina that night. At last they will swallow the bitter drink of their encounter with the devil-possessed bull, Similá Bolosse. As for the men lent to them by Galeona, the one with the pistol will walk in front with the mistress and Jérémie Candé. The others will advance in the order they have already discussed.

Zulé eats with them, chewing the same mouthful a thousand times and looking sadly at Papa Luc, who is no longer even a shadow of his worst days. Then she calls to Jérémie Candé: now old Luc will certainly stay behind. Even if they have to tie him to a post, he'll remain in Jimaguas.

"We won't have to tie him," says Jérémie Candé. "He said he wasn't going."

They calmly finish eating, and Zulé begins to miss the wild songs of Honoré Babiole. She doesn't even have to give the order for everyone to climb into the truck, because when she finally realizes that it's time they have already climbed in, without music and without commotion, exactly as Jérémie Candé has told them to. Then Papa Luc lies down again on his brightly colored blanket, as chilled and weak as a baby pigeon.

"We'll pick you up right here on the way back," Zulé says.

He looks at her scornfully, as if he were looking at a perfect stranger.

"On the way back I won't be here. Besides, how do you know you're coming back?"

They have never kissed, not even in Haiti when they lived at the foot of Mayombe, on the banks of the river that gradually took away the people they loved. She doesn't know how her father's lips smell. And it's too late now to find out.

"Poor Anacaona," says Luc Revé with compassion. "If I die, another Haitian's sure to take her . . ."

Zulé gives a dangerous laugh, the closest thing to a sob anyone has ever heard from her.

"Anacaona's very old, Papa Luc. If you die, nobody's ever going to take her."

Luc Revé laughs too, and that's the last thing they'll remember about each other—those identical sobbing laughs, numb with cold. When the truck finally pulls away, Zulé places her hand under her skirt and briefly caresses the knife Anacaona gave her before she started out on the journey. A long, recently cleared field is the only thing that separates them from the Angelina sugar mill, and a wind dirty with bagasse drives them closer and closer to the vortex. Some of the queens begin to cough, and that is when Zulé distills her final drop of tenderness:

"Shut your mouths . . . Shut them tight and you'll see how you stop coughing."

MALESHERBES MOBIN WAS older than they expected and less taciturn than any other houngan in similar circumstances. When Mistress Zulé and her bodyguard arrived at his house in Loma Copra, a very young woman with crippled feet and a harelip received them but offered no greeting.

"Horns is inside," she said, "cooking his meat."

Zulé asked her to tell him that they came from the Dominican Republic and were sent by Papa Trinidad to discuss very urgent matters with him. They had been traveling all day, it had been very difficult crossing the border, and they wanted to reach Paredón before dark.

"That'll be hard," the woman replied. "Horns is going to eat now."

Loma Copra was a rough, dirty village: a handful of brick houses crowded together in the center, and the others, the majority of the buildings, made of a splintering, weathered wood that constantly had to be shored up. It reminded Zulé of her native Grosse Roche, except that in Loma Copra the people walked as stealthily as cats, gave one another sideways glances, and whispered their greetings as if they were passwords.

"It's because we're right on the border," Malesherbes Mombin explained to them later, "and since the big boss left Port-au-Prince, there's a lot of dirty business in this town."

They had to wait more than two hours, sitting on a dilapidated sofa, until the man with the horns appeared. Life had punished Malesherbes Mombin by placing two gray points, one longer than the other, on the hardened skin of his skull. Zulé had never seen anything like it, and Jérémie Candé, who had seen something of the world, told her that in Puerto Plata there was an Indian who showed anyone who wanted to see, as if it were the greatest prize in his life, an olive green lump that had grown on the back of his neck. He said he didn't cut it off because it brought him good luck and Jérémie thought it was true, but Zulé had her doubts: those horns couldn't grow except through the working of an evil amarre. The discussion ended there because Malesherbes Mombin brought over a stool and sat down in front of his visitors. He had just eaten his meat, and before he said a word he gave a painful belch. He hoped, he began, that Papa Trinidad was well. Zulé lowered her eyes and Jérémie Candé shook his head. Papa Trinidad, the mistress murmured, had been dying for two years and the one responsible was a cruel, savage mambo, Galeona Troncoso, who out of jealousy and spite had put a fatal harm on him.

"I can imagine," said the houngan. "Dominican women are death."

The woman with the harelip came back to offer them watered coffee, and Zulé and her bodyguard gratefully drank the hot mixture. It was growing dark outside, and the houngan lit a small lamp that immediately spewed out black smoke.

"What saint brings you here?"

Papa Luc's daughter shivered almost imperceptibly, and Jérémie Candé, the only person capable of detecting the tremor, looked at her in surprise. A mistress like her, who had been shown the worst hovels by Coridón, felt intimidated by these blackened walls and the little red curtains that partially concealed the back of the altar. But above all she felt intimidated by the lumpy face of Malesherbes Mombin and by his gray horns, gleaming in the dim light.

"I've come to find a Dominican woman," Zulé replied. "They took her from Santo Domingo a while ago and sent her down to the dead. I hear she's in Paredón."

"There's nothing you can do," the houngan immediately exclaimed.

"The family will pay. They want her back no matter how she is."

"There's nothing you can do," he repeated. "Nobody leaves Paredón."

"Trinidad said you could help," Zulé insisted.

"Trinidad knows that all the bokors along the lake are vipers. That's where Similá Bolosse is."

Zulé shivered again, but this time it was a long, visible shudder that ran the length of her body.

"Similá Bolosse is in Boca Chica," she said.

"Similá Bolosse is everywhere. He comes and goes with his macoutes, always doing his dirty business."

They fell silent, and Jérémie Candé looked away, wondering

what they were going to do now. She leaned forward, closer to the houngan:

"There's good money, Malesherbes. Dollars. That woman's husband . . . he wants her back no matter how she is."

"He's throwing away his money," muttered the old man. "Did you tell him what they're like when they come up from seeing the dead?"

"I didn't tell him," Zulé admitted.

"It's bad. That husband will go crazy. The women are worse than the men. You know that, Mistress. Why didn't you tell him?"

She was thoughtful as she waved away nonexistent smoke. Many years ago a serious case had been brought to Coridón. Zulé still remembered the withered face of that girl with the eyes of a fish, and just like a poisonous fish she swelled up like a *poisson fufu* and sprayed everybody with the purple slaver of her venom. Her father, a prosperous Haitian who worked as a gardener in Samaná, spent all his savings to find her on Mont Organisé, where she had been taken after she was put into a stupor. The girl didn't hear or understand anything and was obsessed with putting everything in her mouth, especially the *cul-rouge* spiders that live in the mountains and have such a dangerous bite. Coridón, after looking at the scars on her neck, poured a glass of rum for the father and advised him to take her back to the place where he had found her.

"Tell the husband to leave his wife alone," Malesherbes Mombin advised as well. "Tell him to leave her in Paredón, tell him there are plenty of women in the Dominican Republic. Living women, Mistress, women who shout when you screw them."

Zulé took out the money. She handed twenty dollars to Horns and promised to give him twenty more when they found the girl.

"There's nothing you can do," he insisted. "I have a feeling they pierced her, and if that's true there's nothing anybody can do."

The mistress hesitated but sensed she ought to persist. She took out another bill and pushed it against the houngan's rough hand.

"Then we'll have to go tomorrow," Horns muttered, suddenly overwhelmed by the weight of his good fortune.

Zulé and her bodyguard were invited to spend the night, and before they went to bed the woman offered them herring soup and casabe smeared with lard. Jérémie took a bottle of Dominican rum from his bag and offered it unopened to Malesherbes. The houngan sat looking at it, then hurried to the altar, poured some of the liquor into a glass, and very respectfully placed it next to the jars containing ammonia, holy water, and viní-viní. On the floor there was a buried red cross and next to it a doll with disheveled hair and no arms or legs.

"Baron Kriminel must have the first taste. He always goes first, that's the way this Baron is."

He sat down again with the visitors and calmly began to drink, joyfully savoring the sharp edge of the rum stinging his chest. When he had consumed almost half a bottle, he stared at the mistress and suddenly asked about Similá Bolosse.

"He stayed in Colonia Engracia," said Zulé. "He came there bitten up by insects, but he was almost cured when he left."

Jérémie Candé shifted uneasily; the mere mention of that devil made him feel as if he were being stabbed in the back. He shook his hands as if to brush away the subject, but Horns ignored him; he wanted to know more.

"Now he's in the Colonia Tumba batey," Zulé added. "He's made seven alliances and he doesn't eat any shit."

"Not shit," exclaimed the houngan. "What that son of a bitch eats is Christians. He's going to eat you all because he does business with the macoutes. He always did."

He took another drink and then said he had known Similá since that devil was in his mother's womb. His grandfather, Estimé Bolosse, died in Dajabón during the massacre of Haitians that took place there in 1937; his father, Dieudonnè Bolosse, lived in Paredón for many years and then moved to Jacmel, where he drowned salvaging metal from the bay. Similá's mother, Belle Suzelle, gave birth to eighteen children but only three survived the seven day sickness. She was a hardheaded woman who had her babies alone, over a washbasin filled with onion water, with no healer or midwife to press her belly. It was a miracle that Similá survived, but he came out twisted.

"He's already killed two women," Malesherbes said emphatically. "The mother of his son, a Dominican woman, he threw her into the water near Caracol."

Zulé was about to say something, but she was distracted by the singing of the woman with the harelip, who was busy inside the house:

> *Kalbas kourant ki poté kou li*
> *bay maré kod . . .*

> (It's the gourd that's on your neck
> for tying the noose . . .)

"She's crazy," Horns murmured, "singing at this time of night."

The mistress was exhausted, and the three mouthfuls of rum she had swallowed bubbled in her forehead with the heat of a burning flame. Malesherbes returned to the subject:

"Have you met Similá's son?"

She didn't even answer; she didn't have to. The houngan already knew the answer.

"When you meet him, you'll know Tarzán Similá is not of this world."

Jérémie Candé's eyes were rolling back in his head, but he made an effort to overcome his fatigue and fixed his drowning gaze on the impenetrable face of Malesherbes.

"He's even worse than his father. He hunts down farmers in Savane Longue, in Malterie, all around there, and then he sells them in the Dominican Republic. If somebody doesn't want to go, he ties a gourd around his neck and drowns him in the Masacre."

Kalbas kourant ki poté kou li
bay maré kod . . .
bay maré koooooooooooood . . .

"Why don't you shut up?" Horns shouted, and the woman instantly stopped singing. "He sells them for twelve or fifteen pesos, or maybe he gives them as gifts to his friends. Tarzán Similá loves to give presents."

Zulé had seen the men brought by force into the cane fields, so eaten by lice, so angry and embittered that not even Haitians who had spent more time in the batey wanted to go anywhere near them.

"To tell the truth," Malesherbes concluded, "all of you and your parents before you were sold. The big boss in Port-au-Prince sold you to cut cane. What difference does it make if Tarzán Similá is the one who sells you now?"

The mistress was collapsing with fatigue and had no intention of tying up loose ends at this late hour. But she was sure that a long time ago, just about the time she came to Colonia Engracia, she heard her uncle say that the big boss in Port-au-Prince sold farm laborers to the big boss in the Dominican Republic. He sold them for eighty-five pesos a head, sometimes less. A great many laborers, thousands and thousands, and when there was no more room for them on the government's sugar plantations, traffickers came from other mills and bought them for less, a handful of blacks here, another handful there, half-dead Congos driven from one place to another like dying cattle.

"And now it's time to sleep," Malesherbes Mombin had to concede when he saw that his visitors, noisily exhaling the violent reek of herring soup, had already succumbed.

The trip to Paredón was long and tiring. They left Loma Copra at dawn, and by midafternoon they were still in Rosec because Horns couldn't find the man who was supposed to take them to the lake. Zulé and Jérémie Candé waited just outside the village, sitting on empty crates lent to them at a ramshackle little café at the side of the road. When they had sizzled long enough in the sun, they finally saw a slow-moving dilapidated car in the distance, trailing a twilight wake of dirty earth.

"You two get in," shouted Malesherbes Mombin, as sour and reluctant as if he were seeing them for the first time.

No LABORERS OR WOMEN, not even the children—nobody in the batey has come out this time to welcome them. Nobody except a pair of Dominican policemen who stop them as the truck heads down the main road. Papa Luc's daughter, as leader and mistress of the Gagá, jumps down and walks resolutely toward the men. One of them steps forward and asks in Creole where they come from. But he hardly gives her time to answer: they don't want any more trouble here. If they're going to fight, they'll have to do it in the cane fields. It's prohibited in the batey. *Ou konpran?*

He speaks the language of the Congos clearly, an argot he learned so he could tell off the blacks; so he could roust them in the canebrakes; most of all, so he could know what they were saying to each other.

"Ou konpran, madame?"

Zulé turns her head and finds that Jérémie Candé is also getting down from the truck to stand behind her, without making noise, without anyone seeing him. She remembers then what Coridón once told her: only cats and the children of Chinese can move like that, as if they were standing on the back of the wind; as if their bodies, by instinct, suddenly lost all their weight.

"*Ou konpran?*"

Zulé shakes her head:

"*M pa konpran! M pa konpran! . . .*"

She shouts this in a powerful voice, elongating the words and modulating them as if singing a song. The police become impatient and one of them, a husky mulatto who hasn't opened his mouth yet, moves away from the group and stares at Jérémie Candé's Chinese face.

"Well, you better start understanding," he says at last. "There's a coal-black Congo out there who's coming to give you all a beating."

Zulé directs her gaze at the houses of the batey and sees a group of women crowded around a shack, observing her from a distance.

"Besides," adds the policeman, "there's a dead man in that house. He just died, and they don't want any music tonight."

"We won't make music," Zulé quickly replies.

"Damn it, you fucking have to leave!"

He stares into the somber face of the mistress and then puts a plug of chewing tobacco in his mouth, a large pungent wad that he slowly shifts with his tongue.

"It's very late," she says, lowering her voice. "My people are worn out; let us stay for the night."

The two men stand stiffly in front of the group, looking at everyone and no one, concentrating on the hypnotic face of the woman who insists most.

"I'll give you two dollars. I don't have much . . . "

They don't soften, but from the way they remain silent, Zulé guesses they'll give in at any moment.

"Two dollars and five pesos. It's all I have."

They know she's lying but aren't going to haggle in front of a herd of tired, drunken Haitians as rabid as drowning rats.

"If you stay," the darker one concedes, "you'll have to go inside one of the barracks. We don't want to see you outside."

Zulé agrees without a word, bending her head with a calculated, somewhat rigid humility, a papier-mâché humility that convinces no one. But at this late hour the barracks are better than wandering the roads aimlessly, at the mercy of Similá Bolosse and his gang of macoutes who are surely waiting behind the sleeping mists of the cane fields.

"They're putting us in a rattrap," Jérémie Candé whispers in her ear. "Don't do it, Mistress, they'll lock us in and won't open the door for anybody except Similá."

She had thought of that too, as soon as the man mentioned the barracks the thorn pierced her, but she has no choice. Go out to the fields to do battle right now, or stay here until dawn with an icy heart, wide-open eyes, and a pistol, the single pistol Galeona's man is carrying, ready to spit out its bullets.

"Shut your mouth and tell them to get out."

The two policemen escort the group to the barracks and watch until everyone is inside. At first it smells to them like a pig's liver when the pig has swallowed a lot of mud before being slaughtered. Then there is a stench of stinking bodies recycled over the months and years, the perpetually sweating eternity of the cane cutters. A few laborers are inside, lying on their bunks, their eyes fixed on a ceiling that holds no memories. The people of the Gagá try to find their places in the dark—the women on one side, the men on the other—and Zulé tells them to talk quietly and not disturb the sleeping men. But frequently she hears them stumbling over the bodies of cutters who have climbed down to lie on the cool ground.

"Mistress, do you have a cigarette?"

She raises the lantern and sees a grotesque reddish face with shipwrecked eyes. The man has the high-pitched voice of an old woman, and he is lying on his back, absolutely motionless, partially covered by a jute sack.

"Mistress, why have you come to the barracks?"

He barely moves his lips when he speaks, and Zulé lowers the light, convinced she has seen enough.

"We came to sleep."

"Sleep is for the dead!"

She orders one of the women to get him a cigarette. The laborer's voice bothers her, but what bothers her even more is that he has interrupted her when she is trying to control her anguish, when she is trying to meditate on her involuntary horror of Similá Bolosse.

"The dead or those who want to be dead . . . Look at me, I'd like to be a corpse. Yesterday afternoon a spider bit me and now I can't even stand up, take a good look at me, Mistress."

The woman who brings the cigarette, Christianá Dubois, the War Queen, gives Zulé a message from Jérémie Candé: the people from the wake are waiting outside the barracks to offer her a glass of clairin and ask her please to hold the déssunin for their dead. Zulé is about to refuse when Christianá whispers the most important part of the message:

"Jérémie says you should go out, he says the police gave permission and the people from the wake can be trusted. The dead man's brother is Honoré Babiole's compadre."

The laborer who is beside her mumbles a litany in which he obsessively mentions clairin, and in the middle of his harangue, for no particular reason, he comes out with a phrase that won't mean anything until later:

"You had no reason to stay, Mistress, not now."

Zulé picks up the pouch, which she had taken for safekeeping when they reached the Angelina, and gropes her way to the door of the barracks. Outside she finds Jérémie Candé eating a can of sardines, and two tearful women accompanied by a man named Télémaque Jacques. Following the introductions, they walk slowly to the hut where the body is lying. According to Télémaque, his brother died after cutting himself on the leg with his machete. The wound seemed to close, and by the time it opened up again, all his blood had rotted. The Dominican doctors, holding their noses so as not to breathe in the fumes, told the sick man nobody could save him with a gash like that. Guillotin Jacques, which was the dead man's name, began to shout, long howls of terror begging them not to let him die. But he passed anyway, and now they were afraid he'd come back and do them serious harm.

"Did you take off his shoes?" the mistress asks.

"We took them off," Télémaque replies. "And we bathed him from head to foot, and we stopped up his nose and ears, tied his jaw, and bound his big toes together. We did everything, Mistress Zulé, we turned out his pockets and put salt on his tongue. What else could we do?"

"You did everything," she repeats. "Everything except for one thing."

Télémaque looks at her out of the corner of his eye, and the women who are with him stop crying. But they have reached the shack, and the mistress, incomprehensibly, keeps her words to herself. The dead man is laid out on two tables that have been pushed together; he is surrounded by black candles and covered from the waist down by a flowered sheet.

"You have to leave me alone," says Zulé, staring at the flickering light on the corpse's face.

Then the widow approaches and hands her a new bottle of clairin.

"Drink all you want," she says, "but make him rest in peace for me."

The mistress nods and takes three enormous swallows.

"I need a rooster," she says. "And a strong man with a good stomach. He has to be a relative."

Télémaque volunteers, and one of the women goes outside to catch a rooster. When everything is ready, the widow and the other mourners leave the shack. Jérémie Candé also stays outside, watching with his slanted eyes as the long night begins to fall. All they can hear inside is the beating of the rooster's wings, increasingly prolonged and frequent, increasingly desperate, and the tireless gasping of one person, whom they suspect is Zulé.

> Koté ou kité kay la?
> Na me lesé yo fé . . .

> (Where do you leave this house?
> In somebody else's hands . . .)

Everyone looks at the widow, who has begun to sing in a voice as full and hard as a man's.

> Guillotin ou alé,
> Guillotin koté ou kité loa-yo?
> Sé na Guiné ou alé . . .

(Guillotin, you have gone,
Guillotin, where have you left your loa?
It's Guinea you're going to . . .)

They hear the final squawk of the bird and a soft, definitive thud, like the sound of a fruit breaking open on the floor. Then silence returns—no wings beating now—enveloped in the fog of the song that the widow sings emphatically in her masculine voice:

A, la trache ki réd, mézami.

(Ah, what agony in my heart, my friends.)

The door of the shack opens again, and everyone stands looking at the secretive darkness inside. The candles around the dead man and the lantern that hangs from the ceiling have been extinguished. Nothing is heard, no one comes to the door, and no one dares go in.

"Jérémie Candé . . ."

It is the voice of the mistress that resounds inside the blackness with an impatient echo.

"Jérémie Candé, bring me a light!"

Jérémie hurries to obey, while the relatives and friends of the dead man remain outside and the widow stands motionless, dark circles under her eyes that look blindly at the door where the world has ended for her. At that moment the stumbling figure of Télémaque Jacques emerges. His shirt is stained with blood, and with his arm he pushes aside a woman who approaches to ask him what happened. He walks without stopping until the underbrush is almost up to his knees, he bends toward the ground, and they hear him throwing up. The mistress comes out after him, sweating and blood-spattered, and last of all Jérémie Candé appears, carrying the headless rooster.

That seems to be the signal for the widow to run in and see her dead husband. Zulé exclaims in a loud voice that she would like to wash, and in a few minutes someone places at her feet a basin of warm water mixed with a potion of herbs.

"Even the water smells of devil to me," she whispers, looking out of the corner of her eye at Télémaque Jacques, who is livid and in pain after vomiting up his soul.

The widow comes out again and she too asks for a little water to wash what remains of her husband. Zulé approaches her slowly and gives her verdict:

"Now you can cry for him," she says. "Now your man has risen."

The other woman begins to sob, as if she had received an order.

"I'm crying for him, Mistress, do you see how I'm crying for him? But you have to help me pray for him."

The two policemen have been walking around the shack: as soon as the mistress and her assistant finish their business with the dead man, they'll have to go in the barracks. Zulé returns to the corpse and observes him with the dull eyes of a duty fulfilled. Then she makes the sign of the cross over him, her fingers wet with holy water, and when she is about to seal his lips, she begins to sing in the husky voice of those who have not slept all night:

> *Mwê kwé nan Bondyé Papa*
> *a kigin tout pouvoua*
> *likreyé siel la ak tè a . . .*

(I believe in God
the Father Almighty,
Creator of heaven and earth . . .)

She would have liked Papa Luc to accompany her in saying the prayer. After all, he is the best reciter of prayers in the bateys, the most sought after man at wakes; as good and gentle as a savanna priest, and as unpredictable and meticulous. But the old houngan has collapsed in the empty fields of Jimaguas, and who knows, he may be returning now, carrying all his sorrow back to Colonia Engracia.

"Let's go now," Jérémie Candé urges her. "The Dominicans want us to go."

She looks up and suddenly feels very tired. Similá is close, closer than ever, a stone's throw away. And yet, for the first time in many days, she has managed to concentrate on her own affairs without being overwhelmed by his inescapable presence.

"It's the police," Jérémie insists. "They want us to get in the barracks right now."

The mistress moves away from the dead man, walks solemnly to the door, and from there she looks for the last time at Guillotin Jacques, his face now at peace: in her soul she thanks him for letting himself be worked so docilely. He has been a good dead man, though he was surely very lustful in life. The widow insists on walking with them to the barracks, and her brother-in-law, Télémaque, who is recovered now, catches up with them and hands the mistress five pesos.

"This is from my brother."

Papa Luc's daughter accepts the offering and murmurs the obligatory recommendations: take the body out of the house before daybreak or another member of the family will die soon; turn the coffin around often as they carry him to be buried so that Guillotin can't find the way back to his house; finally, before covering him with earth, throw a live hen, wrapped in the last shirt the dead man wore, into the grave.

"Draw an indigo cross on the foreheads of his children, and don't let them even smell the river water for many days."

Guillotin's widow, with the ravaged face of one who has had a great burden lifted, gives the mistress a last look of gratitude:

"Now you're the ones who have to be careful," she says softly. "There are some macoutes out there looking for you."

It is the moment Zulé has been waiting for. They have stopped beside the barracks, where the people of the Gagá have been sleeping for some time, mixing their travelers' smells with the rank odors of the Congos. She ought to sleep too, close her eyes long enough so that tomorrow she can open them again.

"You have to be careful with those outlaws," the woman insists. "They're mean, like they've been pierced by the devil."

Zulé looks around to make sure the Dominicans cannot hear her. Then she turns her eyes to Télémaque Jacques and spits out the sentence that has been devouring her heart all night:

"What have you heard about Similá Bolosse?"

He begins to chew on an invisible mouthful, avoiding the ice-cold glance of Jérémie Candé and scratching in the dirt with the tip of his bare foot.

"Nobody hears much about Similá."

But that not much is important. Not much is a great deal at this exhausted moment when nobody knows if that devil will come at them in a surprise attack. Not much is so much that Zulé turns like a wounded animal:

"What have you heard about him?"

"What everybody hears," the widow observes. "Nobody said

anything this afternoon, nobody will want to say anything tomorrow."

With a single gesture Jérémie Candé rebukes Télémaque Jacques. They still don't know what half the batey seems to know. They just came from Jimaguas, see? And before that they were in Los Chicharrones, and before that in Guayabo Dulce, and before that, long before that, they were happy and miserable in the cane fields of Colonia Engracia.

"Where is Similá Bolosse?" Zule's dark voice asks again.

"Who knows where the dead are?"

Guillotin's widow has eyes as round as an owl's and a nose so flat it spills onto her cheeks.

"They say his own friends killed him, the macoutes, who knows if it's true . . . They say he's floating down the Mataperros now with his gut cut open."

> *Kokó li pa gin zorey,*
> *mé l tandé brui lajan . . .*

> (A cunt doesn't have ears,
> but it knows the sound of money . . .)

It is a sharp, rough voice, filtering maliciously through the cracks in the barracks and vanishing in the air like a gentle wisp of smoke. Zulé recognizes the voice of the laborer who had asked her earlier for a cigarette.

> *Kokóoooo, kokó li pa gin zorey . . .*

A thread of rage spills out of Télémaque Jacques's mouth.

"That fucking Congo is trying to insult us."

Té a tí kal,
eritié yo anpil . . .

(The plot of earth is small,
and there are lots of heirs . . .)

"A spider bit him," Zulé recalls, her voice drifting and faint, as if she were talking to herself.

"Nothing bit him," responds Télémaque. "He has savanna leprosy, and he's crazy."

Guillotin's widow moves closer to her brother-in-law and whispers something in his ear. He doesn't reply but puts his arm around her waist, and without mentioning Similá again they turn and begin to walk back to the wake. Jérémie, on the other hand, doesn't dare to touch the mistress and is secretly grateful for the intervention of the Dominican policeman, who walks over to them and swears by his mother that he's through being nice: either they go in like they're supposed to or they get the hell out of the batey. Without saying a word they look at each other and do as he says. Inside the barracks the night still smells of pig liver, and Zulé makes her way to the filthy place where the women of the Gagá are sleeping. The laborer with the swollen face, who hears her approaching, takes up his most dismal song again:

Té a tí kal,
eritié yo anpil . . .

"Let us sleep," shouts the mistress.

"Sleep is for the dead. Didn't I warn you that you had no reason to stay? Didn't I tell you that Similá's only pretending to be dead?"

She collapses onto the jute sack that her War Queen has spread on the ground. Christianá Dubois is a stout, good-natured girl, the living image of María Caracoles, Coridón's wife who died of rabies in the Year of the Deaths.

"I'm awake, Mistress. Did you hear anything about that dog Similá?"

As she asks the question the girl trembles, and Zulé caresses her hair.

"You have to sleep . . ."

"They say they cut him," Christianá persists, "they say the macoutes cut his gut open. That's what the laborers say."

They talk in whispers so as not to make more noise than the man is already making with his songs. The girl, still frightened, curls around the body of Papa Luc's daughter, who kisses her face gently and tells her to go to sleep. But Christianá shudders, tossing with fear on the hard ground: is that viper really dead? The mistress kisses her harder: she should sleep now, tomorrow is a great day, they'll eat roast pork in Boca Chica. Christianá stops asking questions and she too begins to lick the lips of the woman who gives the orders. The barracks smells of tobacco and of a womb in heat, it smells of the cane cutters' belches, and it smells most of all of the liquor the mistress has swallowed. The singer is silent for a few moments, as if taking the pulse of the night. Zulé tries not to make noise, but the sweet breasts of her queen quiver and leap in her mouth like little fish on the shore.

Kokó li pa gin zoreyyyyy . . .
oh, la la . . .

To reach Paredón they had to take a shortcut along a narrow road that led directly to Peligre Lake. For the first time Zulé saw those waters darkened by the distant shadow of the Black Mountains, and she felt a tight, hard anguish lodge somewhere in her throat.

"That pond has some good caymans," announced Obenor Laporte, the man who was driving the car. "Good for eating people."

They drove along the lake for a while, breathing in the dizzying smell of sweetish mud and wet dung.

"They eat chestnut pigs, they eat wild dogs, they eat those creatures just for the taste."

Jérémie Candé lowered his head and the mistress obstinately kept her eyes on the landscape. Neither of them wanted conversation, and Obenor resigned himself to recounting his insights to Malesherbes Mombin, who had already heard them countless times before. Half an hour later they entered Paredón, so similar in every way to Loma Copra, with the same line of squalid, ramshackle houses.

"Similá Bolosse was born here," Horns recalled slyly, and he turned his head to look at the indecipherable face of the mistress. "Right here is where that blessed man was born."

The car stopped to make way for a caravan of women carrying baskets on sun-scalded heads. The houngan, incurious and unhopeful, looked at them out of the corner of his eye.

"They're coming from Thomonde," he murmured. "It's market day there. What they haven't sold by now they won't sell at all."

One came up to the car and leaned her head in the window to offer plantains in syrup, the few she had left in a plastic pail. Horns whispered a few words in her ear and handed her some coins, and she placed one of the plantains on a piece of cardboard before whispering in turn:

"Look for Alix Dolciné. Keep going that way."

The driver stepped on the gas and Zulé felt some apprehension.

"We're pretty close now," the houngan remarked.

They drove on in the direction the woman had indicated and only found an old woman gesticulating in the wind and talking to herself. Horns jumped out of the car while it was still moving and asked for Alix Dolciné.

"I'm Alix Dolciné," the old woman replied without looking up.

"Listen, I have some gourdes . . ."

"Gourdes aren't worth anything. Don't you have dollars?"

Malesherbes Mombin, struggling to control his impatience, put his hand in his pocket and took out some of the money Zulé had given him the night before. Then he spoke very quietly to the old woman, who kept brushing away the swarm only she could see.

"It's complicated," said the houngan, returning to the car. "We won't know till midnight if it's her."

Jérémie clenched his jaw and Zulé snorted in exhaustion. They still had many hours to wait in Paredón, and the best thing, Horns suggested, was to go to the lake and have a glass of rum. Obenor Laporte turned the car around, tires squealing, and a short while later they stopped in front of a stand made of planks where a woman was fanning a dark broth of blue shellfish.

"Crabs," exclaimed Zulé, overwhelmed by the weight of a distant smell, a taste of childhood that sharpened her submerged memories of the river near Mayombe.

They asked for rum and sat on some crates that they placed near the shore. The woman brought them a can of boiled crabs, and Malesherbes Mombin began to break them apart with his fingers and suck out a few dark scraps of meat, tasting of mud.

"Eat the eyes," he advised Jérémie Candé. "They're good for your seed."

Zulé pretended not to hear, and Obenor mumbled another story about the proximity of caymans.

"For your seed and for your brains," Horns said emphatically, obsessively rubbing his two points. "Similá Bolosse always ate them." An ominous silence fell, and they could hear the water lapping against the rocks. "I swear to God, when he was little he didn't have anything else to eat. But when he grew up he had almost everything: pink pigs, boiled turtle, iguanas . . . And still that devil kept eating these crabs."

"Now he eats people," declared Obenor, tearing at an unyielding mouthful with his teeth.

When it grew dark they moved away from the shore. The

woman from the stand came over to warn them it wasn't a good idea to stay near the water.

"The caymans bite," she whispered, pointing at the mangroves, and Obenor looked at all of them with the foolish smile of a man who has made a lucky guess.

They sat down under the palm leaf arbor and continued drinking until the woman announced she was going to close. There were no doors or windows, and they all understood that closing meant putting out the fire and carrying away in a bag the only two bottles she had left. Obenor was drunk, nodding to himself and murmuring disconnected phrases, but since no one else knew how to drive the old jalopy, they resigned themselves to zigzagging down the wretched road that brought them back to the center of town. Not a soul was to be seen on the streets of Paredón, and it was so dark they almost ran over Alix Dolciné, who was punctual, livid, and sorry, she said, that she had ever gotten involved with Dominicans.

"Not a single Dominican here," Horns protested, while Obenor leaned against a tree to vomit up his liver.

The old woman made a face and said that nobody could accompany her to the place where they were going except the mistress and the houngan from Loma Copra.

"The drunk and the Chinaman have to stay," she said, pointing at the two of them.

Obenor did not understand completely, but all the same he went to the car to lie down on the eviscerated backseat, and immediately fell asleep. Jérémie Candé made a silent promise that he would follow Zulé, even if it had to be at a distance, but Alix Dolciné read his heart:

"Not at a distance and not up close. Nobody goes except the ones I say."

They began to walk out of the village, heading for the part of the lake called Black Waters. The old woman led the way, almost running through the underbrush, indifferent and deaf to the cries of Malesherbes Mombin, who could barely keep up with her. They went on for some time, guessing the direction the old woman took by the distant echo of trampled leaves, and smelling more and more distinctly the water's swampy stench that merged occasionally with the frontal stink of carrion.

"Now you wait till I get back," shouted Alix Dolciné, unexpectedly appearing at their back, as if she had been following them.

"We'll wait," Malesherbes Mombin replied submissively.

Zulé felt dizzy. A faint taste of vomit and rum festered at the roof of her mouth, and the fetid odor rising from the water almost took her breath away. Lightning flashed in the distance, among the blurred peaks of the darkest mountains, and nearby, just a few steps from where the old woman had left them, they could clearly hear the sound of scorpions fighting.

"Papa Bolosse is watching over his flock . . ."

It was the changed, hoarse voice of Alix Dolciné, speaking to them from her hiding place behind some bushes. Horns responded by breaking into a wretched smile whose crumbs scattered in the darkness, and then he found his smallest voice, crucified by meekness:

"For Papa Bolosse we also bring his due."

Zulé stood motionless, afraid to open her mouth. But she managed to ask if Similá had returned from the Dominican Republic.

"Bull Belecou never leaves here," thundered the old woman, stamping on the interminable battle of the scorpions.

At this point, Horns thought it prudent to learn the whereabouts of the woman they were searching for.

"She'll come down to drink in a while. But I don't think anybody can take her away."

"Well, that's what the mistress is paying for," replied the houngan, "to take her away from here and back to her husband . . . Is she that bad?"

Alix Dolciné burst into laughter, quiet little yelps that merged with the vivid noises of the night.

"Hell, the Dominican's fine. And she'll get better: she'll give birth in silence the way snakes do. Isn't that good for her husband?"

Zulé felt as if the ground were suddenly opening in front of her. The women who went down to the dead never made a sound again, not even to shoo away chickens, and they didn't even groan when they gave birth to their babies, whether they had ten or whether they had twenty.

"If she's pregnant, we won't be able to take her," Malesherbes Mombin said with a discouraged sigh.

"The husband wants her no matter how she is," Zulé insisted. "If she's pregnant, then I'll take her pregnant."

Alix Dolciné laughed again, and the houngan called Horns, who had struggled half his life with the silent flocks of Peligre Lake, took the mistress by the arm and said from his heart:

"Don't hope for anything . . . It can't be done by force."

Two days of traveling, so many dollars wasted, so much weariness, an awful trek and all for nothing. Zulé squatted down and remembered what Coridón had often told her: there was some work not worth getting involved in. And when a woman went down to the dead it was better to let her stay. Because the deep swoon quickly clung to her bones, she had seen it with her own eyes, and the swoon could not be removed even when her own death came.

"Papa Bolosse is in his houmfort drinking Bermúdez rum."

Zulé raised her head and looked up at the monstrous face of Alix Dolciné. Until that moment she had not considered the real presence of Similá, there behind the scrub, drinking the Dominican rum that the legions of Congos liked best.

"Papa Bolosse is waiting for you."

They heard more scuffling between scorpions, and then the sound died away on the shore, hissing and sputtering like a submerged torch. The mistress stood, brushing off her dress:

"Similá will have to give me that woman."

Alix Dolciné cleared her throat, spat noisily, and changed the tone of her voice again:

"Papa Bolosse doesn't like to wait. And he doesn't like people making demands."

Then the three of them plunged into the underbrush, wrapped in the devilish wind blowing off the lake and in Alix Dolciné's perverse song:

> *Lac la fond,*
> *morts you dessan'n vi'n*
> *souce lan'm vag yo . . .*
> *Kité scorpions yo,*
> *nan Peligre guin place pou toute moune.*

> (The lake is deep,
> and the dead come
> to drink their own passage . . .
> Move the scorpions aside,
> Peligre Lake has room for everyone.)

A SHORT WHILE LATER she falls asleep and has a long dream about the dead man at the wake. Guillotin Jacques is not Guillotin Jacques but Similá Bolosse. And Similá Bolosse is wearing large two-toned shoes that move together in the dark. All the dead have big feet, Coridón once told her. Perhaps that is why, in her dream, Similá's feet are still growing while she desperately tries to remove his shoes, knowing that if a dead man is buried with his shoes on, he'll disturb the peaceful sleep of the living with the sound of his footsteps.

"Mistress, it's Sunday."

Jérémie Candé makes his way to the place in the barracks where the women of the Gagá are crowded together and shakes Papa Luc's daughter, who sleeps with her arms around the blue-black body of her War Queen.

"We have to get going . . ."

She dreamed about Similá Bolosse, that much is certain. But now she'll have to see if she can remember the rest. Her mouth still reeks of clairin, and the warm breath of the girl who sleeps beside her smells fatally of her own breath.

"Mistress, we're waiting for you outside."

It is growing light, and she shudders with a momentary sense that she may be continuing the journey to nowhere begun in her dream. But she soon realizes this is useless: she cannot turn back now, she cannot flee, she cannot avoid the fixed stare of dawn. Christianá Dubois, still stupefied by her recent pleasure, opens first one eye and then the other, then closes them both and stretches, her body marinated in the nocturnal saliva of the woman who licked most.

"We have to get going," the mistress repeats, swallowing the ashes of a foreboding that eludes her memory.

"Today we'll eat pork," the girl exclaims, as if they were speaking in two different places.

It is the first Easter Sunday in many years that dawns with claps of thunder, and over the Angelina a dirty rain is falling that gives no sign of stopping.

"What have you heard about Similá Bolosse?"

Christianá stops abruptly. What can anybody have heard about that animal except that they cut open his gut and threw him in the Mataperros River? Zulé begins to dress and only then recalls the man who sang all night. She turns her head and sees him there, motionless on his bunk, the jute sack pulled up to his shoulders, the rotten guava of his profile barely visible. She would like to sing now too; it is the custom on Easter Sunday for the mistress to sing for her Gagá. Too bad she can't even open her mouth; if she does, a water snake might slither out that could poison the whole Societé. She can't sing and she can't think, and the stale taste of clairin comes and goes between her lips like a living fish.

"Today we'll eat pork," repeats Christianá. "And go down to Boca Chica; we're going down, aren't we?"

Christianá is animated and looks without dismay at the funeral mask of the mistress's face. Zulé finishes dressing and finally goes out to the empty field where two of the elders are busy arranging a green canvas over the truck that will take them back to Colonia Engracia that night. Jérémie only has to look at her to know the world has collapsed.

"It's going to rain all day," he calls from a distance. "We're putting up a cover," and he points in vain at the green canvas, which Zulé ignores, just as she ignores the perfect formation of the Gagá, the solemn tone of the drums, the woeful melody of the bamboos, one of them singing alone like an animal bidding farewell to the night.

She continues walking, as if those people didn't belong to her; she passes the last houses in the batey and jumps across the nearby open sewer, a leap that almost tumbles her into the filth. The air smells of decay, it smells of cane fields and the boiled cane blossoms used to prepare tisanes for curing urinary ailments. Zulé doesn't think, she doesn't look back, she doesn't feel or suffer. In a frenzy she crashes into the plantain grove and tears off her clothes, her skin scrapes against the sticky trunks, and she falls into an uncontrolled fit that ends in a trance, and the trance in death. Half the Gagá has run after her, and Jérémie Candé, devastated and sad, is the first to reach the scene of calamity. He shakes her shoulders, he breathes into her face, and sprays on her chest a few sips of kimanga first warmed in his own mouth. The mistress does not respond but bellows in confusion and breaks her nails clawing at the stones on the ground. Christianá Dubois, with the raw intuition of those who never think, finally manages to quiet her.

"Don't cry, Mistress. Similá can't be dead, that devil's just fooling us."

Jérémie Candé raises the bottle again; this time he doesn't warm mouthfuls of liquor to dampen the perspiring chest of Zulé but takes two murderous swallows instead. Sprawled on the ground, barely covered by the embroidered cape of one of her elders, the mistress trembles the whole length of her body. Christianá cradles her head and kisses her eyes, and Papa Luc's daughter, forsaken and alone in the midst of her own people, weeps for the pain of a love she didn't weep for during three years of despair. Jérémie returns to her side and observes her recovery as if he were observing the resuscitation of a drowned dog, with the same lack of pity, almost with indifference.

"Now I know why you never let me watch . . ."

Zulé hears him as if in a dream, but even so she can grasp the categorical tone of his words.

"You covered over the cracks, Mistress, but I heard you. Even in Papa Luc's house I could hear you howling, you and the dog Similá, when you were fucking."

Christianá tells him to shut up. Papa Luc's daughter is suffering a great mounting, you only have to look at her eyes or hold her hands, ten fingers that are no longer Zulé's fingers but those of the angry mystery who rides her. He'll have to bring rum, rub her between the legs, then let her crawl wherever she wants to go. Or doesn't Jérémie know that she's the mistress of the Gagá? Has he forgotten that in the Colonia Engracia batey the reddened prick of Ogún Ferraille burns in obedience to her? Doesn't he remember that the fierce beings in the sacred Palm still come down to eat in the Vevé she prepares for them? Jérémie is too engrossed to listen to the harangue of an arrogant girl who learned only yesterday about the untamed soul of the mistress.

"You shut up," he says, "what do you know. . . ?"

Christianá looks at him with the enthralled expression that precedes the birth of great hatreds.

"You stay out of it," Jérémie Candé shrieks. "How many times did you sleep with her? Only last night, before yesterday you never slept with her, what do you know?"

The elders are more united than ever; the musicians haven't experienced greater harmony in many years; and the queens, always proud and quarrelsome, have never been so affectionate with one another. But the Gagá is fatally wounded and Mistress Zulé doesn't realize it; the mistress only has the courage to open her eyes wide, swallow the earth that has stuck to her lips, and stare at the dripping canopy of the plantain grove.

"What have you heard about Similá Bolosse?"

A silence like stone descends and controls those present. Papa Luc's daughter, miraculously pulled from the vengeful jaws of the river at Mayombe, is about to drown in the shallow waters of a small pond.

"Similá is out there," Christianá prods her. "If you don't get up, he'll tear us all to pieces."

"We have to go back to Jimaguas," she murmurs. "We have to get Papa Luc."

During these days of wandering through the bateys, Jérémie Candé's hair has begun to grow back. The stubble of his lank, lifeless hair is something that irritates his hand when he rubs his skull, something he finds repugnant at times.

"Get up, Mistress . . . let's go cut off Similá's balls."

Jérémie is astonished at the boom of his own voice, he

scratches his head feverishly, as if it were crawling with lice, and in the same menacing tone tells one of the elders to give him the wooden cross he wears around his neck.

"We have to get Honoré Babiole too," Zulé continues. "If Galeona lets him go."

"First we cut off Similá's balls," Jérémie Candé insists. "First him. Get up!"

He pulls at the mistress so unexpectedly that nobody has time to intervene. This is not the first time Jérémie has been ruthlessly mounted, but it is the first time he has dared to attack Zulé during a trance. Two elders immediately come forward to restrain him, and Christianá Dubois, convinced that Papa Luc's daughter is in danger, heroically covers her with her own body.

"Kiss the cross!" Jérémie is beside himself. "Kiss the cross, damn it . . ."

You don't need to be an adept to know he is possessed by Carfú. Only a mystery like Carfú demands something like that from his mount, and the leaders of the Gagá sense that before long Zulé's bodyguard will start butting his head; start ordering them to serve him pork and squash on the same plate; start pleading with them to mix his meat with dirt. Carfú loves the sacramental taste of roads.

"Bring more rum," shouts the mistress, getting to her feet, recovered and free of the weight of her own loas. "More rum for Carfú so he'll let us return, so he'll free us from the shadow of Similá Bolosse."

Confusion reigns in the Gagá. It is almost noon, it is Easter Sunday, and instead of returning to the batey they are trapped there, witnessing a fight to the death between loas who see the field wide open and come down to hold their own festival.

"More rum! Carfú likes rum!"

Zulé has come to her senses and Jérémie doesn't stop crying.

"A black handkerchief, somebody give me a handkerchief . . ."

It is still thundering, but the heat is infernal inside the grove. Jérémie extends his arm so that the mistress can tie on the handkerchief handed to her by one of the musicians. They are so close to each other that when they sniff the air they both perceive the odor of misfortune. Zulé smells of sweat, the sweat of centuries that clung to her bones when she left the barracks, and Jérémie smells of gunpowder, he smells of massacre, suddenly he smells of fried meat. When the handkerchief is tied on tight, his eyes wander and he thunders in a voice not even remotely his own:

"Similá, here we are."

All the members of the Gagá, all of them at the same time, have the same presentiment. They are surrounded; they feel as if they were stripped naked before eyes that have been observing them since daybreak; they are defeated even before they locate the bloodthirsty face of the man who is soon discovered:

"Look, it's Similá!"

Christianá Dubois, War Queen, is the one who gives the alarm. She doesn't have her red flag with her, but to declare a war declared so often, she doesn't need it. There's the dog, there's the devil, there's the wordless snake, alone and slippery with poison. There he is at last, the mad bull, the most criminal criminal in a long line of criminals.

"Ah, Similá," brays Jérémie Candé. "This isn't your road, boy."

The bokor of Paredón doesn't even bother to answer him; he is too intent on the movements of Mistress Zulé. She advances to a point halfway between her own Gagá and the group of villains commanded by Similá Bolosse.

"Move away, Zulé," shouts a voice that comes from the throat of Jérémie Candé but belongs a thousand times over to the irrascible rider who is mounting him. "Move away and go with the women."

Those possessed by Carfú tend to weep copiously but also demonstrate the power of their arms by going to the countryside and butchering brutes. Jérémie Candé, who is now Jérémie Carrafur, who is the same as Carfú Coridón, who is the devil Guedé on his mother's side and the devil Guedé on his father's side, raises his right hand, shows his middle finger to Similá Bolosse, and shouts the war cry that rebounds among the dripping bunches of plantains:

Vin chita sou ça!
Similá . . . vin chita sou ça!

(Come sit here!
Similá . . . come sit here!)

THAT SONG TOLD the truth: in Peligre Lake there was room for everybody. And as they walked toward the houmfort of Similá Bolosse, Malesherbes Mombin was telling Zulé that the lake was as big as the ocean and the waters near the shore as thick and warm as snail soup. They walked hand-in-hand, following by instinct the trail of Alix Dolciné, who sometimes vanished in the darkness but knew all the hiding places along the way with the enthusiasm of someone who sooner or later will disappear into them. The old woman was still singing when they reached the bokor's hut, and she stopped only to ask at the door if they could come in. A voice Zulé had almost forgotten answered yes, the three of them could come in, and Malesherbes Mombin, when he recalled the moment afterward, said it hadn't been like entering a houmfort but like falling headfirst into the caverns of a bad dream.

Similá Bolosse didn't look up but Zulé didn't have to see his face to know he was cured of all his wounds. She remembered the last time she had seen him, walking away from Colonia Engracia under the white shower unleashed by the parrots.

"They keep telling me about you," said Similá, a touch of irony in his voice.

"I sent a message asking you to help me," Zulé reproached him.

"You don't want an alliance," Similá reminded her. "So I can't help you."

Malesherbes Mombin stood to one side, enjoying the glass of rum that Similá had offered him.

"You're not a grateful man," Zulé insisted. "I helped you when you came to my batey. Now I'm the one who needs you. You have to give me the Dominican."

"She isn't in my flock," replied Similá.

"You can still help me. If she isn't with you, she must be working somebody else's land."

"I don't know . . . I can't know everything."

Zulé lifted her arms to pull back her hair, showing her damp, dark underarms, like two large open sexes, to the big boss of Paredón.

"One of the bokors around here must know. You're all the same."

"The same as what, Mistress Zulé?"

She spit out her soul:

"The same as the devil."

The glass slipped out of Malesherbes's hand, and Similá Bolosse made his big yellow eyes flash.

"Horns, in this houmfort you don't spill rum . . . Which loa are you offering it to?"

Horns shook his head and picked up the pieces of the glass that had broken on the floor in a strange way, as if forming stars.

"Rum isn't spilled here and neither is blood."

Similá couldn't hide his irritation, but still he tried his best to discourage the mistress: if she took away that woman and gave her back to the husband, she'd have to tell him where she had found her. What would she say to the Dominican then? How would she defend herself when the police came asking questions?

"They never thought she was with the dead," replied Zulé. "She just disappeared, that's why I dared to come."

"It's all the same, Mistress. What's the difference? In the Dominican Republic everybody knows they took her down to the dead."

Then there was a long silence. Similá didn't ask when they would leave, he didn't even bother to say good-bye to Malesherbes Mombin, among other reasons because Malesherbes simply evaporated, he slipped through a crack in the night. Old Alix Dolciné had left the temple despondent but soon returned in great excitement to say that a woman, possibly the Dominican they were looking for, was in a group of living dead who had come down to drink water. Similá Bolosse stood up with the deliberateness of a man who has everything decided, and Zulé noticed that the bokor of Paredón was stouter than she remembered.

"Let's go take a look at her."

He didn't wait for a response from Papa Luc's daughter. He pulled her along by the hand, and in the dim light of a lantern they walked toward the place along the lake where they could hear a sound of lapping as intense as twenty cows all drinking at the same time. Alix Dolciné caught up with them and whispered to Similá that the way was clear. The man from Paredón kept pulling at the mistress's hand, and she felt her feet sinking into the sand on the shore and into the warm pools left behind by the surge of water. At last he stopped and raised the lantern as high as he could; it didn't cast much light, but it was enough for Zulé to see the cloud of shadows moving away into the underbrush. Only one, a spectral figure tinged with blue, remained squatting on the shore. Similá brought the lamp close and used his most threatening voice:

"Let me see you."

The woman did not move. Instead, she seemed to grow more compact, hardening around herself like a snail in its shell. Similá picked up a branch from the ground and buried it in her hair.

"Stand up."

The woman remained motionless, and the most diabolical bokor in the region lost his temper, whirled the branch around, and twisted it into her tangled hair. Then he pulled back the stick, moved aside her Medusan locks, and revealed her pale features, the staring eyes, the permanent rictus of a woman who has gone down to the dead.

"Get up, bitch!"

She had to make a great effort, but she struggled to her feet and Zulé discovered that the woman was less mulatta than she had thought; she was almost white. Then Similá raised the woman's face even higher, using the same branch, and for a long time he looked at the unprotected face that kept trying to turn away from the light. The next thing he did was to throw cold water on the seething head of the mistress:

"They worked her eyes and must be using her for seeing and telling. Now you have even less chance of taking her away."

Zulé remembered, in a single blinding flash, what worked eyes meant: the liquid landscape teeming with the dead, the heart-rending agony of the apparitions.

"This one's eyes are shining," said Alix Dolciné, reappearing abruptly in front of the bokor, shooing away the invisible flies that swarmed around her, and making the sign of the cross three times in a row, over and over again, in the presence of the torpid monster. "Looks to me like somebody gave her salt."

"The husband wants her no matter how she is," Papa Luc's daughter repeated faintly.

"The way she is now not even her own shadow wants her," Similá Bolosse declared conclusively, lowering the lantern.

The mistress would have liked to see her a little longer, find out if in fact this human ruin could detect the same things she had seen long ago, when Coridón agreed to sharpen her eyes. But the man from Paredón took her by the arm again and pulled her back to his houmfort, not without first stopping near Alix Dolciné, still lost in her conjectures:

"Though it probably wasn't salt . . . Maybe something went wrong when they dug her up."

A creature who had gone down to the dead passed through several stages, but sometimes its sleep was damaged from the start, from the very instant it was brought up from below. Then it couldn't be used for carrying messages or planting crops and was slowly consumed in the muddied dark of its own somnolence.

"I know you came with the Chinaman," Similá said after a while. "But he has no guts . . . Coridón wasn't careful where he put his seed."

Zulé responded halfheartedly.

"Coridón knew what he was doing. Not me, look how I'm losing my money."

She was overwhelmed then by the certainty that she really had made this long trip for nothing; or perhaps it was to confront for the last time the proud soul of the man who had forgotten too quickly his sufferings in the countryside, the stabbing pains of savanna sickness, and the night he had miraculously survived, feeding on the untameable breast of the woman who loved him most.

"Now you're telling the truth," the bokor declared with conviction. "You don't know what you're doing . . . Look how you turn down alliances; look how you order the cutters not to let us come through Colonia Engracia; look how you stir them up so they won't let us stop there. That's why you're losing your money."

It was so late and Zulé was so tired that she heard his words as if through a veil of water. When they reached the houmfort Similá undressed her with no preliminaries, sprinkled her with the viní-viní water he used for his work, and pushed her toward the bed, a cot covered with old feathers, many of them stained with blood, which the mistress did not even bother to brush aside.

"The day I left Colonia Engracia, the parrots left too, didn't they, Mistress?"

He embraced Zulé without anger and without passion, waiting for the response of that woman who made only one instinctive movement, only one, to make certain no one was watching them through the cracks.

"The parrots didn't leave," she said with a sigh. "They just stopped making noise."

Her memory burned less than the searing reality of Similá Bolosse; her memory was much lighter than the weight of that body slithering painfully on hers.

"Why do you want war?" Similá whispered in her ear.

"I don't want war," panted Papa Luc's daughter. "But I don't want an alliance either."

"No, don't want a war. Remember I always win them."

Then the bokor of Paredón stopped speaking, coiled around the nourishing flesh of the mistress, and buried his fury in a deep digesting sleep from which he did not waken even when Zulé slipped out of bed to open the door. It was already light outside, a rainy day, and the mistress could see the dripping figure of Alix Dolciné, accompanied by Malesherbes Mombin, Obenor Laporte, and Jérémie Candé.

"I've been calling you since dawn," said the old woman. "It's time you people left."

Horns had moved away from the group, as he always did whenever he smelled danger. But Obenor Laporte and Jérémie Candé stood as if hypnotized, looking at Zulé's reinvigorated body.

"Get dressed," the old woman managed to say. "And no noise, because Similá Bolosse had a very hard night."

Some feathers were clinging to Zulé's chest, and Obenor Laporte gave a dry little chuckle and remarked harshly:

"That bokor hasn't cleaned his houmfort for a long time . . . Those feathers are from the chickens he offered to Lokó Atisou on other nights."

"That's nothing," Alix Dolciné cackled. "He's keeping goat balls in the pot for boiling coffee."

"He must be making a macho paquete," Obenor Laporte speculated.

"Sure he is," replied the old woman.

"And they must have ordered it from Port-au-Prince."

"Sure, Obenor, but how do you know they need paquetes in the Palace?"

The sound of a crash that shook the pilings of the shack interrupted this exchange of hunches. Zulé looked at the old woman and Obenor Laporte, then saw the distorted face of Malesherbes Mombin, and missed only the vengeful face of Jérémie Candé, who, as usual, had slipped away without anyone noticing him. Then she had a premonition that left her paralyzed in the doorway, and Alix Dolciné, who had the same premoniton at the same time, forgot for a moment about shooing away her flies and shoved past the mistress to get inside. They all followed her in, just in time to keep the all-powerful black Chinaman from strangling to death Similá Bolosse, who was naked, with his tongue protruding, and dazed by the mists of a nightmare he could not escape.

"Let him go, you bastard!"

It was a woman's voice, but none of the men in the temple could tell if the order came from the impassioned throat of Alix Dolciné or Zulé.

"Let him go, compadre, you're burning up alive . . ."

The warning from Malesherbes Mombin did the rest. Jérémie loosened the pressure of his fingers and Similá fell to the ground, coughing, writhing, cursing Ogún Balenyó because he had abandoned him to wild dogs that had come from the Dominican Republic.

"Go!" shouted Alix Dolciné. "Go now!"

Zulé dressed blindly, her staring eyes fixed on the bokor of Paredón who was still clearing his throat and spitting out the acid spume of his fear. She and her men walked the long distance to the car in silence, and before beginning the trip back to Loma Copra they stopped to watch a flock of mangy buzzards flying in a circle over the waters of the lake. One dropped in a nose dive and Obenor Laporte said he'd be damned if that bird hadn't seen the meager remains of a woman's body. Zulé understood him immediately: the Dominican she had hunted for so long was dead, dissolving in the waters of the same treacherous pond where she usually went to drink. A second buzzard dropped straight down after the first, and Obenor Laporte, watching it dive, intoned the song for putting babies to sleep:

> *Ti zoazo koté ou pwalé?*
> *M pwalé kay Fillete-lalo.*
> *Fillete-lalo kon'n manjé ti mounes;*
> *si walé la manjé ou tou.*

> (Little bird, where are you going?
> I'm going to see Fillete-lalo.
> Fillete-lalo eats little children;
> if you go, she'll eat you too.)

Obenor continued singing in his funereal voice until they reached Rosec, and there he disappeared from view, not without first concluding that the caymans of Peligre Lake were not the caymans its bokors were. Jérémie Candé had not exchanged a single word with the mistress, and the mistress refused to look at him even when they were alone, after they had said good-bye to Malesherbes Mombin, who did not invite them again to Loma Copra but serenely summarized the incredible outcome of their trip.

"You people are done for, Mistress . . . That bokor has a tough hide. Give him an alliance, give him help in your batey, give him whatever he asks for. And pray he doesn't kill you when you go out again with your Gagá, pray he doesn't start a fight so he can cut your soul in two."

"You're very stupid," Zulé said to Jérémie Candé after they crossed the border. "I thought you could kill him."

Livid and enraged, he looked at her and chose to be silent,

reached the outer limits of silence, remained silent in spite of everything with the obstinate faith of despair.

"But only a real man could have killed him," she concluded, looking at his crotch. "And Similá is right about one thing: Coridón didn't know where to put his seed."

A MOMENT COMES WHEN Similá Bolosse's yellow eyes multiply insanely around the plantain grove. It is the moment when the face of the world darkens, as if night were falling in the middle of the day. Jérémie Candé, alias Papa Carfú, keeps his finger raised in order to provoke Bull Belecou, alias Similá Bolosse. Mistress Zulé, standing on the line that divides their fury, looks first at the murderous face of Coridón's son, then searches the scrawny jungle of plantains for the feverish face she once licked out of pity and licked again because she liked the fire. When Bull Belecou becomes aroused, the entire earth seems about to open, and when Similá Bolosse decides to raise his voice, a hot fetid air descends on the plantain grove:

"Let's negotiate, Mistress Zulé."

The words come out of his throat with a double echo, as if he were speaking in chorus, as if Bull Belecou, in his infinite rancor, wanted to intensify the bitter gall of his words.

"But tell that bigmouth to get lost."

Christianá Dubois, the War Queen, stands in the middle of the stifling heat and lets loose a torrent of words, attempting to summon Ogún Badagri, lord of altercations. She screams her invocation in the sultry air but no one dares to mock her. Not even the people from the batey, huddling on the far side of the grove and waiting in silence for the fight to boil over. Similá Bolosse, as is customary in these cases, has paid the plantation guards to be deaf and distant.

"Jérémie is my First Elder. I can't take him out of here."

"Your First Elder was your father, but I think your father died. Then it was Honoré Babiole, and I think he's going to die too. Don't provoke me, Mistress, get that fucking Chinaman out of here!"

"He's mounted . . . don't you see he's mounted by Carfú?"

Jérémie keeps shaking his middle finger and pointing it at Similá Bolosse. From time to time he laughs, demands more rum, and mutters a tongue twister that no one in the Gagá ever heard him say before.

"To hell with his mounting. For the last time, Mistress Zulé, I'm offering you an alliance or a war. But if you want us to talk you have to get that son of Coridón's evil seed out of here."

Like a bolt of lightning, like a spark igniting her memory, at that instant Zulé recalls the ragged voice of the houngan of Colonia Azote when he gave her his warning. Coridón, at the point of death, had asked her to marry Jérémie Candé, and when she refused he advised her to be wary of the one who would come later, to be very wary about backing down before the bastard with three balls.

"This is my territory," Zulé thunders. "My Gagá has always come through here . . . You took a route that wasn't yours."

"Aaaaaaaah, Mistress Bitch, since when does a whore set the route for a macho bull?"

Zulé's elders move forward in disarray, making threatening gestures and forgetting the formation that Honoré Babiole prescribed for starting the battle. Papa Luc's daughter, following her own impulses, puts her hand under her skirt and pulls out her knife. Similá Bolosse, the great animal of the countryside, better known as Bull Bolosse, fierce lord of the world, raises his machete and spits out three of the filthy words loved by angry gods. A handful of his men, who are clearly macoutes, begin to move too, their eyes fixed on Zulé's elders. At their head marches Tarzán Similá, the image of his father, sprinkling the air with the white powder he carries in his pouch.

"Come try my finger, Similá . . . Let's see if you have the balls!"

Jérémie Candé grabs his crotch, rearing up and dropping down as if he could not touch bottom.

"I have more than I need," is the bokor's icy reply. "Just ask your mistress."

A gust of wind and rain passes over them, and the men quiet down momentarily, intimidated by a bolt of lightning that crackles among the leaves. The elders of Zulé's Gagá stand a few steps away from the treacherous elders of Similá Bolosse. Nobody has pulled out pistols, nobody boasts about them, but Bull Belecou keeps waving his machete as he walks toward the rigid figure of the great Carfú. Similá crosses slowly in front of Zulé, and she doesn't have time to smell the reek of that body swelling with pride, the same body that once left Colonia Engracia, covered in the white tufts of betrayal.

"Jérémie Candé!" the mistress shouts at last. "Get out of the grove!"

Coridón's son no longer answers to his name, even though it is Zulé who is calling him. Carfú Candé bucks and snorts all around Similá Bolosse, eluding the intense whirling of the machete, hunching over to avoid being slashed.

"Similá . . . let's cut off each other's balls!"

The man from Paredón, as sure and rapid as an eel, steps back in order to make a better assault.

"Get out of here," Zulé insists. "Get away, Carfú, Jérémie Candé, get away. Let me negotiate with the bokor."

Then a strange storm is unleashed, as if the rest of the loas, to placate the warriors, presented them with a hailstorm to distract them for a second, only a second, from the sorrow of their journey. But the cloudburst does not hide the light. It rains while the sun shines and that is the devil's work, and the mistress gently rebels in a voice that does not even resemble the one she had until that day, a voice borrowed from the great metresa who is going to mount her.

"Take away Jérémie Candé," she orders two of her elders. "Take him away to the truck."

Christianá Dubois, drenched and trembling, watches with bulging eyes as the men face the difficult task of dragging Jérémie away from the plantain grove. Zulé turns to the bokor and says the few key words of an afternoon from which there is no return:

"Now come fight with me."

Similá laughs, he laughs with joy, nobody has ever laughed as much as he does.

"Are you going to want an alliance?"

The mistress is soaking wet. Down her tear-streaked face streams the muddy water that filters through the vast canopy of the plantain grove. Her crown is heavy, and when she attempts to remove it she howls in pain and looks at her bloody hand. In an unlucky moment she forgot the razor trap concealed there by Lino the Haitian.

"Are you going to want an alliance? Are you going to let my cargo pass through your shitty little batey? Are you going to let me use the barracks of your Congos?"

The rain comes down harder and Zulé assumes it must be raining fishes in Colonia Engracia; she even thinks she sees her stepmother Anacaona, bending over the ground, intent on gathering up sardines before the puddles are lapped again by the sun.

"Are you going to want an alliance or do you want more war?"

Papa Luc's daughter, her knife in the air and her hair loose, looks more than ever like the metresa Erzulie Freda, a hot whore with a deep heart, a lover of perfumes and white food, of everything made with flour and everything that smells of milk. The saints say that the metresa Freda insisted on trying the seed of Bull Belecou. But Bull Belecou humiliated her, he mistreated her at night and obliged her to drink the white urine passed in those days by black snakes.

"I don't need pistols," Similá taunts her. "If you want war, I'll give you some machete."

Erzulie Freda decided to take her revenge. She walked in the night and searched the countryside for the most untameable of all the loas, the one called Belie Belcan; she offered him a kid, which is what he likes best, and asked him to work a crushing harm on Bull Belecou. Belie Belcan accepted her offering and promised he would bring her the blood of that bull. But the truth is he never kept his word.

"But you, Mistress of Trickery, you like to shoot bullets. You went to Galeona Troncoso, you asked for her men and left her that moron Honoré . . . Does Honoré Babiole know I gouged out his brother Truman's eyes?"

Zulé starts to walk toward the bokor, as docile as if he had offered her a yellow drink, a menthol cigarette, an enormous black prick, everything the metresa Freda likes best.

"You ought to make an alliance, Mistress Zulé. We'll live together in Colonia Engracia or the Colonia Tumba batey. And in the Dead Time we'll go to Peligre Lake to watch over the flock. What's your answer, Mistress?"

She cannot help imagining Anacaona's horror so far away as she roots around the purple guts of the opened fishes, trying to divine the future in the icy entrails that will tell her everything before anything happens.

"Hurry up, Mistress, I'm running out of patience."

Papa Luc's daughter throws away the knife and stops abruptly in front of the bokor.

"I'm not going to break my Gagá. It's the Gagá I inherited from Coridón."

"You don't have to break it. You and I will make it great."

She feels dizzy and looks down at her bare feet, spattered with the blood running down from her hands. The hard image of Anacaona returns to her head, crazed with horror this time, seeing in the fishes everything the mistress cannot see inside the grove: the slashed back of Erzulie Freda, her gesture of love before the scornful image of Bull Belecou, her ignorance of the movement of the blade that comes from behind, gently slicing through the underbrush.

"Carfú!" howls Anacaona in her house in the Colonia Engracia batey, and her howl startles the Gagá of Elías Piña in Guayabo Dulce; and Lino the Haitian in Manoguayabo; and Honoré and Galeona Troncoso in La Cacata; and old Luc Revé, more dead than alive, in the warm refuge of his brightly colored blanket in the Jimaguas settlement, a step away from the Angelina.

"Carfúuuuuuu!"

Zulé also hears the shout and turns around, but she has no time to be startled. The machete comes down, brushing her cheek, plunging into her neck, and in passing cutting off the tip of her nipple. She raises an arm to protect her face, and it is the second blow of the machete that slices off at the root those fingers that twitch on the ground like living worms. After he sees that she is motionless, Jérémie Candé drops the machete and looks at his blood-spattered hands. Tarzán Similá, driven mad by the smell of blood, races over to him and destroys his knees. Coridón's son falls down, overcome by pain, and begins to slither between the trunks under the sleepy gaze of the bokor, who sees everything without moving.

Inside the plantain grove nobody understands anything. But Christianá Dubois, the War Queen, in an effort to comprehend the world, kneels at the foot of the corpse, and though she knows no one will pay attention to her, she calmly begins to scream.

"MY HANDS ARE SHAKING . . ."
Anacaona washes Zulé's body with the meticulous slowness of someone cleaning a slaughtered animal. She has begun at the bottom, scraping the souls of her feet and putting a small white towel between the toes to wipe away the dried blood; then she moves up her legs, rubbing the knees that were never the same color as the rest of her body, that were always gray.

"I washed her when she came to the batey, and I'm washing her now that she's leaving me."

The first time, the water in the washtub gleamed with greasy muck. Now there is no washtub, no screams from that wild little girl begging to be set free; Zulé is quiet, lying on two tables pushed together, showing no sign of running away or biting the arms that hold her down; she cannot hear her stepmother's soothing song.

Osanyo, lamizè pa dous,
agoé.

(Osanyo, misery is not sweet,
agoé.)

Anacaona's voice is overwhelmed by her weeping, it is a voice that breaks and dies away as she begins to clean the glorious groin of the mistress, her blue pubis, the wrinkled, desolate lower belly that all corpses have.

"She liked going naked. She looked like a Haitian."

She rubs her arms, covers the purple hole where her nipple had been, and without really knowing what good it will do, sprinkles her hips generously with talcum powder.

"Help me dress her."

When she was alive it never would have occurred to Zulé to wear so much under her dress. Now, in addition to underwear, Anacaona has put dark flesh-colored stockings on her, held up by garters above her knees. She is going to lay her out in her own way, refined and well-dressed, and for that she needs the help of Luc Revé.

"Lift her head."

She perfumes her temples and ears and combs her unconquerably kinky hair, which is stiffer and darker than usual.

"Now let her rest."

Papa Luc's hands are shaking too, especially when he pulls them from under the ice-cold nape of Zulé's neck. Wiping his eyes, which filled with tears when he heard the song, he sits down again in his rocking chair.

"The bukán is still burning," Anacaona remembers. "Somebody has to put it out."

Only then does the houngan realize that the obligations to the saints have not been met, and until they are, the beings of the Palm, who are three, Ti Jean Petró, Erzulie Zeux Rouges, and Ogún Ferraille, will keep rumbling around the batey. From the corner where she lies curled up in a ball, Christianá Dubois, the War Queen, proposes the unthinkable:

"Let it go out by itself."

"That can't be," Papa Luc exclaims. "It has to be put out and our obligations must be met. I don't want the mistress to torment me."

If the Gagá had returned unharmed, if Zulé had survived, all of them would have already gathered around the flames to burn their sticks and crowns, singe their clothes, and put out the fire, not without first thanking the mysteries for their protection in allowing them to come home safe and sound.

"But the mistress came home dead," Christianá says. "Who will we give thanks to?"

Outside, the people of the batey are attentive to the business of laying her out. The shack is so small that in order to say goodbye to Zulé they will have to pass through one at a time, and Anacaona, who does not want to disturb the great sleep of the one who suffered most, comes to the door and imposes her rules:

"Nobody touches her. You look, you cross yourselves, and you go on your way."

It is dawn on Monday, and the cane cutters are waiting for the overseer's bell to set out slowly for the fields. The women will spend more time at the wake, until it is time to prepare lunch and carry it out to the canebrakes. Anacaona and Papa Luc already know that in the long run they will remain alone with the broken vessel of Zulé's body. Perhaps Christianá will decide to keep them company. Perhaps she will stay.

"The war with Similá was bad," Anacaona murmurs as she watches the endless line of mourners pass by.

Papa Luc, his eyes half-closed, smells the intense odor of honey and tallow given off by the black candles.

"He bathed in the blood of a hundred good goats. Have you ever seen a hundred goats all at once?"

The old houngan doesn't respond. For the first time in many years he is thinking about his first wife, Zulé's mother, and about the two sons he lost in Haiti. He always thought his only daughter would die by water too. In a sense, he hopes she has.

"Similá cut off their heads, he bled them all, and then he got into the tub and offered it all up to Lokó Siñaña. When he came out he was on fire, even the whites of his eyes were red . . . the same red as the red of his shadow."

Some men try to shake the withdrawn hand of the houngan, and when they realize it is pointless they touch his shoulders and caress his chin. Before they leave for the fields, two of the elders offer to nail the coffin shut. Christianá Dubois rushes out of her hiding place, kisses the lips of the mistress, and immediately moves away, as if she had swallowed a mouthful of poison.

"It seems that Lokó Siñaña is a grateful loa," says Anacaona, raising her voice above the sound of the hammers.

"It seems that way," replies Papa Luc as he gets to his feet.

GLOSSARY

Agave: a plant with fleshy leaves that have thorns around the edge and on the tip. A fiber used for making rope is obtained from these leaves. The plant is commonly called "cowtongue."

Amarre: a name ordinarily used to indicate a certain kind of spell.

Bamboos: tubes of bamboo that produce the low tones characteristic of the music of the Gagá cult.

Baron of the Cemetery: a member of the Voudon pantheon who rules the dead and resides in all cemeteries. Along with Baron Samedí, he belongs to the terrible family of the Guedés, who are spirits or loas strongly linked to death and all its manifestations.

Batey: an area containing workers' houses and barracks on the outskirts of the sugar mill.

Bokor: a Voudon priest. He differs from a houngan because he works with both hands, that is, with the forces of both good and evil.

Bower: a primitive construction of wood and palm leaves where most of the Gagá's ceremonies take place.

Bukán: a ceremonial fire represented by an iron bar. It is fed with rum and gasoline.

Casabe: a cake made with flour extracted from cassava root.

Central Post: poteau mitan in Creole. A sacred stake located in the center of the Bower; the "mysteries" come down the stake and gather there.

Clairin: Haitian liquor.

Déssunin: a ceremony by means of which a person's corpse is separated from the loa or spirit that has ruled it in life.

Elders: male members of the ruling hierarchy of the Gagá; their number varies between ten and thirteen. The first has more prestige than the others.

Fututos: shells used to call together the members of the Gagá.

Gagá: a socioreligious form of worship practiced by Haitians and Dominicans in the sugar-growing regions of the Dominican Republic.

Gourde: the currency of Haiti.

Guedé: the Lord of Death, or a group of spirits linked with death.

Houmfort: a Voudon temple.

Houngan: a Voudon priest.

Kimanga: a ritual Voudon drink.

Lamé: the person who leads the Gagá's pilgrimage, clearing the way with a whip.

Loas: the entities or "mysteries" who rule the Voudon pantheon; in a trance or possession, they ride or "mount" the head of an individual, who is called the "horse." The loas can be either Radá or Petró.

Majá: a very large yellow snake. It is not poisonous.

Mambo: a Voudon priestess.

Metresa: a feminine loa or deity belonging to the Radá division of the Voudon pantheon.

Palm: the sacred palm, also called "white," the supposed residence of the entities who protect the Gagá. Its location is a secret known only to the master or mistress and his or her closest associates.

Paquete: a kind of protection enclosed in a container resembling a large onion and topped by a cross. Paquetes are either male or female, depending on their contents and purpose.

Petró: a group of strong and powerful loas or "mysteries." They differ from the Radá in their love for iron, fire, and glass, and in constantly brandishing a machete.

Protections: small bags generally made of goat skin and filled with certain substances that protect the wearer from harm and bring good luck.

Queens: women who hold high positions in the Gagá.

Raising: a ceremony that is part of the rite of initiation into the Gagá. The initiate is literally elevated in a chair.

Seed: a red spot in the yolk of an egg. By extension, in some parts of the Caribbean, it is a name for seminal fluid.

Tamboras, Tambúes, Tatúas: musical instruments played to enliven worship and to summon the "mysteries."

Toque: the playing of ritual drums used to invoke the loas. Each loa is invoked by a distinct drumming.

Vevé: ceremonial drawings made with corn flour, ashes, and coffee grounds. They represent the nature of the "mysteries" or loas.

Viní-viní: a liquid frequently used in many of the rituals typical of Dominican Voudon. Magical properties are attributed to it.

ABOUT THE AUTHOR

Mayra Montero was born in Havana in 1952 and currently lives in Puerto Rico. She is the author of the novels *The Messenger*, *In the Palm of Darkness*, *The Red of His Shadow*, and *The Last Night I Spent with You*, all translated from the Spanish by Edith Grossman.

ABOUT THE TRANSLATOR

Edith Grossman has translated the poetry and prose of major contemporary Latin American writers, including Gabriel García Márquez, Mario Vargas Llosa, and Alvaro Mutis.

Atlantic Ocean

Mayombe Hill

Grosse
Roche

HAITI

Paredón

Peligre
Lake

Caribbean
Sea

———— Route of Zulé's Gagá

·····················> Route of Similá's
drug shipments